A MAN FOR
AMANDA

Other Books by Jane McBride Choate

A MAN FOR AMANDA

•

Jane McBride Choate

AVALON BOOKS
NEW YORK

Published by Avalon Books,
an imprint of Thomas Bouregy & Co., Inc.
New York, NY

Library of Congress Cataloging-in-Publication Data

Choate, Jane McBride.
    A man for Amanda / Jane McBride Choate.
        p. cm.
    ISBN 978-0-8034-7460-4 (hardcover : acid-free paper)
1. California, Northern—Fiction.   I. Title.
PS3553.H575M36 2012
813'.54—dc23

                                        2011033936

PRINTED IN THE UNITED STATES OF AMERICA
ON ACID-FREE PAPER
BY RR DONNELLEY, HARRISONBURG, VIRGINIA

To Amanda Cabot, sister of my heart

*And to Lia Brown, for her belief in this book
and her invaluable help with it*

Chapter One

"Darn it, Harry. Get out." A woman's voice carried down the narrow hallway.

Lucas Reed had just stepped into the old-fashioned foyer of the boardinghouse. Instincts honed from over a decade on the LAPD had his muscles tensing, his hand reaching for the .38 he no longer carried.

"I told you I didn't want you in here."

Lucas cursed the bum leg that kept him from moving faster. He dragged his right leg behind him.

The woman didn't sound desperate so much as exasperated, but fear did funny things to people. He didn't have his piece, but he figured he could still take out Harry Whoever-He-Was.

He shouldered open the door and burst into a kitchen. Habit had him going in low. Trouble was, he no longer had a partner to take the high road. Pain slammed into his rotator cuff before he pushed the thought aside.

A woman turned astonished eyes in his direction. She

stood at an old-fashioned sink and directed a narrow-eyed glance his way.

It took him a moment to register that her assailant was a large, floppy-eared dog who regarded him with a goofy smile from a face that was half-black and half-white. Paws on the kitchen counter, he sniffed at a plate of cupcakes.

"Lucas Reed."

"Amanda Clayson."

"Harry?" he asked with a glance at the dog. His heartbeat, which had spiked, smoothed out, returning to its regular rhythm.

Almost.

"I'm sorry," she said with a wave of a flour-covered hand. "Harry loves cupcakes. Won't leave them alone. Would you take him out? I'll be with you in a minute."

With the hapless Harry in tow, Lucas beat a retreat. The woman must have thought him crazy, bursting into her kitchen like some parody of Dirty Harry.

What did they say? You could take the man out of the cop shop, but you couldn't take the cop out of the man.

Amanda cleaned up the best she could. She sponged off as much of the chocolate from her shirt as possible and thought of her initial meeting with Lucas Reed. So much for making a good impression on her newest boarder.

Reed was a writer from LA. The dust jacket of his latest book, which she had propped up on a shelf to read whenever she had a spare moment, showed a hard-faced man with startling blue eyes and an unsmiling mouth. It was the face of a man who'd seen too much of life, most of it bad. His bio stated that he'd spent twelve years in the LA Police Department.

She'd read all his books and found them well-crafted, gritty, and depressing. She wondered about the man who chose to make his living writing about the darker side of life. She took another look at the book jacket and studied his face once more. It mirrored both of his professions—the action and the intellect.

What would his presence do to the cozy family atmosphere of Sweetbriar? She couldn't afford to think of that. Quite frankly, she needed the money his rent would bring.

Money. The Bible had branded it as the root of all evil. Those more learned in the Good Book would tell you that it was the love of money that caused the problems. Amanda didn't love money, but she did need it.

She found Lucas waiting for her in the parlor. He filled the small room with a restless energy that was not diminished in the least by his limp.

He crossed the room and took her hand in his. "Sorry about that. I thought . . ." He shrugged, a self-deprecating gesture that drew her attention to the breadth of his shoulders.

She smiled. "No harm done."

His answering smile was wary, as though his lips were unaccustomed to the upward movement.

An arc of awareness shimmered between them. Strange, she thought, that a simple meeting of palms could produce such a jolt.

Little ripples of response skidded down her spine even after he released her hand. The back of her neck tingled, the tiny hairs there standing at attention. Tension shimmered in waves so intense that she was startled the air didn't pop with electricity. For a moment, she'd imagined something had passed between them, something more potent than physical attraction.

She spared a moment to enjoy the sensation. What normal woman wouldn't? Lucas Reed was drop-dead gorgeous. He could have graced the cover of one of the romance novels she kept by her bed.

What made the whole experience so unnerving was that she hadn't felt the least physical interest in a man since she'd ended her engagement.

Lucas hunkered down to scratch Harry between the ears. "So you're the culprit."

Harry quivered with pleasure at the attention, turning a sloppy tongue toward its source.

Amanda felt bound to defend Harry. "He's really a sweetheart. He just has this thing about 'helping' me in the kitchen. He's a good watchdog," she added.

Lucas looked doubtful. She couldn't blame him. Harry took a little getting used to, with his mismatched eyes and seriously ugly face. She'd had a few bad moments herself when Florence Wanlass had shown up with the huge dog who looked like he could devour both of them in one bite.

Lucas rose and grimaced. There was no missing the way he favored his right leg, the slight limp seeming out of place in his rangy, athletic build. It didn't detract a whit from the power that emanated from him. Nor did it lessen the nearly overwhelming attraction she felt.

She took her time studying him. In person, his looks were even more arresting than on the book jacket. Hair so dark it was nearly black emphasized a square-jawed face. Black jeans, a matching T-shirt, and well-worn sneakers completed the look.

His face was all angles and planes, lined by the sun and the life he'd led. She searched for some hint of softness. And found none. It was the face of a man who had faced his demons and triumphed but not without a price, a lived-in face made all the more attractive by the struggle.

There was something that drew her gaze back to his eyes. They weren't cold but hurt. She doubted he was even aware of the pain that shadowed them. He looked like he needed to learn how to laugh. She wondered if she would be the one to help him.

Just what I need, she silently jeered, *another stray to care for.* Her sisters had teased her mercilessly about her strays: an abandoned cat, a gerbil her friend couldn't take with her when her family moved, a sparrow with a broken wing. Amanda's strays, they'd called the small creatures she'd brought home with her on a regular basis.

Lucas Reed, she couldn't help noticing, didn't look helpless or abandoned. In fact, he looked darn near perfect. He was a prime example of the male of the species.

"Finished?" he asked.

Caught staring, Amanda flushed, then smiled. "Yes."

"Do I pass?"

She cocked her head to the side. "I don't know. I'll let you know when I do." She was flirting with him, she realized with a start.

Remembering her duties, she gestured around the high-ceilinged parlor. "Everyone's welcome here. There's a TV and plenty of chairs." She wrinkled her nose. "Be careful of the springs on that," she said, pointing to a horsehair sofa. "Harry's usually the only one who sits there. You're welcome to do your writing here if you start feeling claustrophobic in your room."

He nodded.

"Help yourself to anything in the kitchen. We normally take meals together, but you can have yours in your room if you prefer."

She led him to the wraparound porch. "This is my favorite place come evening."

Florence Wanlass floated to the porch and enveloped her in a Shalimar-scented hug. "Amanda, introduce me to the stud-muffin."

Florence, swathed in a dozen or more scarves and sporting a purple bejeweled turban on her head, stood six feet tall. A few stray curls, currently a flaming red, peeked from beneath the turban like errant children playing hooky. Broad of hip and voluptuous of bosom, she had a heart to match her generous proportions.

Amanda performed the introductions.

Florence inspected him much as she would a ham at a butcher's shop. "You're better-looking in person than on your book covers."

Lucas chuckled. "Thank you, ma'am."

"No thanks required. I call 'em as I see 'em. You're going to liven things up around here." She patted Amanda on the shoulder. "Amanda here needs someone besides Rudy and me. You look like you could stir her juices and set them to boiling if you had a mind to."

Amanda assured herself she wasn't going to blush. Just like Harry, Florence took some getting used to.

"I remembered what I came to tell you. The washer is rumbling again," Florence said.

Lucas knew he shouldn't ask, but the question came out anyway. "How does a washer rumble?"

Amanda sighed. "It belches out suds and water."

That didn't sound so bad. A little soap and water. He was about to ask if she wanted him to have a look at it, but she was already gone.

His leg didn't allow him to move very quickly, and he struggled to catch the words that drifted through the open door as he followed her. He grinned as her language grew more creative.

Cautiously, he pushed open the door to the kitchen. A green monster of a washing machine advanced toward him. "What the heck—?"

"Save yourself," she said. The grimace on her face told him she was only half joking.

He winced as his sneakers squished through several inches of water, but he didn't retreat. No matter—he couldn't let her face the runaway washer by herself. He got behind it, reached for the plug, and jerked. The washer hiccupped its way to an uneasy silence.

"Thanks," Amanda said. "I thought it was going to get me this time for sure."

" 'This time'? You mean, it's done this before?"

"Yes." She shrugged. "It acts up about once a month or so. This was the worst, though."

"What do you intend to do about it?"

She looked surprised. "Wait till it's cooled down and then finish the laundry."

"You're not going to use it again?" He'd faced knife-wielding gangbangers who didn't scare him half as much as that runaway washer.

"I have to." She smiled. "Its bark's worse than its bite. Once it's rested, it'll be fine."

He had the feeling of having stepped into an alternate universe. "Washing machines don't need to 'rest.' Not normal washing machines."

She rewarded him with another one of those smiles that threatened to turn him inside out. "This isn't a normal washing machine. It's one of a kind."

"Thank heaven," he muttered under his breath.

"They don't make 'em like this anymore," she said, patting the machine fondly.

"They haven't made them like this in the last fifty years," Lucas said, eyeing the green beast warily. "It belongs in a museum. The Smithsonian would probably pay good money to put it in their Early Americana exhibit."

"Well, they can't have it until I finish my laundry."

"What if something else happens?" he asked, his forehead creased with worry.

"Like what?"

"Like it blows up and hurts someone."

Her smile was unconcerned. "I'm the only one who uses it. Besides, it won't blow up. It just likes to spit and sputter a bit."

Her lack of concern for her safety made him angry. "All the more reason to replace it."

She started to push the machine back against the wall. Lucas set her aside and finished the job.

With what he considered foolhardy courage, she plugged the beast back in. It sputtered briefly before settling into a contented hum.

She turned to him and smiled. "My hero. Thank you. You'd probably like to rest. I'll show you to your room."

He didn't move.

Guileless brown eyes met his with an inquiring gaze. "Is something wrong?"

He shook his head, unable to answer. The lady was a witch and had put him under a spell. That was the only answer. There was no other logical reason for why he had spent the last few minutes wrestling with an antiquated washing machine and then feeling he should apologize for maligning it. Lucas believed in logic, in the hard-and-fast rules he lived by.

A cop to the bone, he checked out his surroundings, noting the jumble of clothes, piles of cookbooks, the rainbow of sticky notes on the walls. He winced. How did anyone function in such chaos?

His shoes squeaked as he followed her. He looked down at them and wondered if disarming a renegade washing machine might find its way into his next book.

She led him up a winding staircase, showed him to his room, and told him to call if he needed anything. A crocheted tester covered the bed. Hooked rugs were scattered over the hardwood floor. Layers of paint filled cracks in the plaster ceiling like an old woman's makeup trying to disguise wrinkles. Pine beams crisscrossed the high ceilings. The faded wallpaper complemented the muted colors of the rugs.

The effect was at once inviting and soothing. His lips curved wryly. Sweetbriar was a far cry from his normal haunts, which featured cold drinks and warm sand.

He unpacked and wandered downstairs, then outside, and took his first good look at the Victorian house. It had probably been a showplace a century ago. Now it showed its sags and scars, rather like an old lady not afraid to act her age. It rambled in all directions, the result, he supposed, of haphazard additions over the years. Rather than detracting from the structure's character, they added to the charm.

He shifted his gaze. To the west, the mountains stood as nature's sentinels before they sloped gently into foothills. He turned and saw gray-green fields undulating far into the horizon. An apple orchard flanked the south side. A barn, painted the requisite red, loomed to the north. The scent of animals wafted through the afternoon air, exotic to his city-boy senses.

He found Amanda hanging clothes on a line in the backyard. A straw hat shaded her eyes against the sun, casting her face into shadow so that he was startled by the brilliance of her smile when she looked up at him.

"Don't you have a dryer?" Why this sudden interest in laundry? The lady who cleaned his condo took care of his laundry as well.

"No." She shoved a bag of clothespins into his hands. "Hold this." She stretched a sheet over the line and pinned it into place.

"Hanging clothes to dry . . . that's obsolete."

She repeated the process with a second sheet. "I prefer to think of it as environmentally conscious."

"Wouldn't it be easier to use a dryer?"

"A lot easier." There was a shrug in her voice that made his concern seem out of place. "Unless you happen to find a couple of hundred dollars lying around, I'll keep doing it the old-fashioned way."

He followed her with the bag of clothespins, feeling like a bee drawn to an exotic flower. He tried not to notice the softness of her skin as his hand brushed hers and the sweet scent of freshly laundered sheets tantalized his senses.

Amanda had no qualms about drafting her newest boarder. She figured he'd let her know if he objected to hanging clothes. Until then, she wasn't going to turn away an extra pair of hands.

A thimble-sized breeze rustled his hair, blurring the edges of his side part. She felt her heart give a nervous jerk. Her breath stuck in her throat, and she sucked in a lungful of air. At the same time, she felt curiously breathless. She inhaled deeply, needing to clear her mind.

The aloofness that normally distinguished her was swamped by awareness of a man. This man. Perhaps it was the expression in his eyes that said he had come to terms with who and what he was. It was an appealing brand of self-confidence that contained only a trace of arrogance.

His lips turned upward, and she realized he knew she was staring at him . . . and wondering. She didn't want to feel breathless around him, to go all weak-kneed and tingly. She certainly didn't want her pulse to pick up speed and lose its steady rhythm.

The last thing she needed in her life at the moment was a man.

She threw back her head, and a breeze caught her hat and tossed it to the ground. She bent to reach for it at the same time as Lucas. Their hands touched, lingering for a moment before pulling away.

He straightened. "I . . . uh . . . I think I'll go boot up my computer."

She gave an absent nod. "Dinner's at six."

She thought of what had brought her to this place.

When Aunt Roxy had left her the house in the foot-hills of northern Colorado, Amanda had grabbed at the chance for a new life. She'd spent too much time marching to the beat of someone else's drum, too many years trying to conform her lifestyle to that of her family. Working at a job she hated, attending the right social functions to further her fiancé's career, patronizing the right stores hadn't come close to the life she wanted.

She'd dumped her job, traded her power suits for jeans and killer heels for sneakers and her near-ulcer for sunshine. She hadn't looked back. She felt like she'd been born again.

The big, rambling house had faulty wiring, antiquated plumbing, and no central heat. Still, she loved it with a passion that had been altogether lacking in what she'd felt for her erstwhile fiancé.

She'd used the small inheritance to remodel the bedrooms, install a new furnace, and add a second bathroom. The rest would have to wait. Until then, she was content. Or, she would be, as soon as she solved her money problems. Property taxes on the house and adjoining land were due in two months.

Turning her inheritance into a boardinghouse had been a business move. Naming it Sweetbriar seemed a natural, given her love for all things sweet, especially chocolate.

Her elderly boarders had become her family, if not of blood, then of the heart. She couldn't see them go without, even if it meant sacrificing some of her own wants. And a new washer, she told herself firmly, was just that. A want. It could wait. The old one had served Aunt Roxy well for more than forty years.

She had done her homework, created a Web page, and opened for business. Her two elderly boarders were dears. They'd quickly made a family and had embraced Amanda just as she had them. She realized she needed them as much as they needed her.

Aunt Roxy would have approved. As always, when Amanda thought of her aunt, a smile slipped onto her lips and into her heart. Aunt Roxy had never lived her life according to someone else's dictates. She had embraced life, squeezing out every bit of pleasure.

Amanda liked to think of her aunt in heaven, thumbing her nose at anyone who dared to tell her what she was supposed to do, just as she had on Earth.

On the other hand, her great-aunt may have gone in the other direction. Either way, Amanda expected her to be issuing orders rather than taking them.

Her family had never approved of her great-aunt. Aunt Roxy's name was spoken of in hushed tones.

Amanda had adored her. The only true grief she'd ever known was when Aunt Roxy had died—with no fuss or warning. She'd been eating ice cream in bed. Double fudge, of course.

She'd left the house, the farm, the orchard, and a prized collection of recipes to Amanda. To her nephew, Amanda's father, she left her wishes that he find something to smile about before they met again. To her niece-in-law, she left an ugly garnet brooch, because it was the only thing she could think of that Loretta had ever fully approved.

It had been so like her, Amanda thought with a pang, those pithy little comments in the will. Aunt Roxy had lived her entire life in the rambling house, content with her orchard, her gardens, her friends.

The letter Aunt Roxy had left her was imprinted on her mind.

Dear Amanda,

   Use the farm for whatever you want. Don't march your way through life. Dance with a pink feather boa floating about your shoulders. Above all, be happy.

Love,
Aunt Roxy

It was typical Aunt Roxy. In your face and full speed ahead. Amanda didn't think Aunt Roxy would mind the mixed metaphor. Her aunt had been a rebel long before the hippies and feminists had had their say.

The only problem was that Amanda wasn't a rebel. She was a homebody, a homemaker, and that was the biggest rebellion of all.

She loved cooking, drying herbs, making a home. The house and farm and animals that went with it healed her in ways she hadn't known she needed to be healed.

She figured she was a throwback to another age. Not that she didn't appreciate the choices that her mother and others like her had made possible. It was just that she chose to make a home.

Amanda didn't need a great deal. She never had. She preferred thrift stores to boutiques and home cooking to restaurant meals. Only the expectations of her family had kept her working at a job she hated and living in the city. She had shed her old life like a snake shedding its skin.

The household where she'd spent her childhood had been a model of organization and efficiency. Never a home. Cushions were plumped just so. No footprints marred the perfection of the plush carpet.

There'd been no magazines scattered about, no personal mementos, no casual snapshots tucked into books.

Only one stiffly formal family portrait, replaced every year, gave a hint as to the people who lived there.

No one was allowed in the kitchen outside of the cook and the maid. It, too, was a showplace with its state-of-the-art cookstove, Sub-Zero refrigerator, and glossy tiles.

To Amanda, the house had been a trap.

Aunt Roxy had bucked the family tradition and had lived as she chose, had said what she thought, and had always, always had a place in her heart for her great-nieces.

That Amanda's sisters had rejected her love and her lifestyle had been a heartache, but she'd never reproached them, had only directed her considerable love toward Amanda.

Living in Aunt Roxy's house symbolized a change of course. In one direction lay the life her family had pushed her toward, a life devoid of joy and full of the *should*s and *ought*s that characterized their own carefully ordered existence.

In the other direction lay freedom. There were no guideposts, no expectations to fall short of, no well-meaning people who wanted what was best for her—as long as it was their idea of what was best.

There was only herself. The realization was both exhilarating and sobering. For the first time in her life, she was doing exactly as she wanted. If she fell on her face, there'd be no one to blame but herself. And no one to share the credit if she succeeded.

Her mother had accused her of betraying the feminist cause when Amanda had turned from her former life. In truth, Amanda had no desire to bump up against the glass ceiling of the corporate ladder.

Her gaze shifted to the rolling foothills surrounding the orchard. When she'd been a child, she'd imagined the ancient apple trees muttering complaints to one another as they huddled together against the winds that blew down from the mountains. She was a child no longer, but she still liked the look of the gnarled and knotted trees, marching in neat rows.

The sun-deepened green of the pines in the woods spread a sleepy peacefulness over the hot August afternoon. It was that scene that had snared her attention all those years ago when she'd first come here as a small child.

Things had gone downhill in the subsequent years. As she'd adopted her family's values, made their goals hers, her visits to Aunt Roxy's farm had grown fewer and fewer.

When she arrived a year ago, bruised from her broken engagement, she had winced at the run-down condition of the place. The paint on the outbuildings and the fencing had nearly worn off, and the house looked as if it had been neglected for years, but that sense of timeless peace had still saturated every foot of the place.

How she had needed that peace.

She cut her meanderings into the past short. She had work to do. It wouldn't get done by taking a stroll down memory lane. With the laundry basket under her arm, she headed inside.

The wacky cake she'd promised Mr. Goldblume was next on her list. Her Aunt Roxy's recipe, the cake had no eggs but the unlikely combination of baking soda and vinegar, and, of course, a generous dose of cocoa. She assembled the ingredients and began mixing.

Inexorably, her thoughts strayed to Lucas, and she wondered if he liked chocolate cake. Somehow, it seemed important that he did.

Chapter Two

Sunset in the mountains was nature at its best. The sun was riding low in the sky, bleeding fiery light. The mountains were dipped with color. Greens and golds. Blues and purples. If he were an artist, he'd find a way to capture them on canvas. As it was, he had only words.

And they had dried up.

Mere words were inadequate to describe the beauty stretched out before him. The quiet was unbroken. He was besieged by color, the richness and thickness of it. Heat still clung to the day, but he felt a bit of the evening cool.

He had no use for sunsets, no matter how spectacular. He had come here to work. And, maybe, if he were lucky, to save himself.

Lucas made his living spinning yarns, and a very good living it was. His last book had sold for a cool three million. There was even talk of a movie deal, with him writing the screenplay. Not bad for an ex-cop with a bum leg.

The money had never meant anything to him. It was simply a way to keep score. He supposed the cynical attitude was a by-product of his years as a cop.

He was more fortunate than most. Other retired cops took jobs as security guards or night watchmen. More than a few discovered they had no life outside the job. He had a career that provided opportunities most people only dreamed of.

He had everything.

A condo in the right part of town. The right clothes. The right car. A flourishing career.

And he had nothing.

His condo was too new, too pretentious, the parties to which he was invited too shrill, the women he dated hard, brittle, and grasping.

Through it all, he was desperately trying to find himself. The Lucas Reed who had started out so many years ago with youthful ideals and untarnished dreams, the man who had vowed to make a difference in the world.

That man no longer existed. He had done more than burn out. He had disintegrated with the death of his partner, Danny. His shattered leg was only the excuse for leaving the force. Not the reason.

Danny echoed through every feeling, every thought, every decision. It had been in Danny's memory that Lucas dedicated his first book.

The reviews had labeled him "an ex-cop with a flair for words." Yeah, that was him. A poor excuse for a cop who got his partner killed, then wrote a book about it and made a boatload of money.

The more successful he grew, the greater his self-loathing. He'd set up a trust fund for Danny's kid, a pistol of a boy who had his father's gray eyes and easy smile. Danny's wife had been grateful, embarrassingly so. She'd never blamed Lucas. Perversely, he wished she had. He could have handled her condemnation better than her forgiveness.

Not surprisingly, the thought of Danny put a weary ache in his heart. More out of practice than desire, he ignored the great empty place where his soul had once been and focused on the present.

He had a little less than three months in which to write his next book. His publisher was growing nervous, giving the little signs that publishers do when a deadline looms and no manuscript is in sight.

An ad on the Internet had caught his attention. Sweetbriar advertised itself as a boardinghouse in a mountain setting offering a unique dining experience. The name itself intrigued him.

Years on the force had honed his instincts. He'd learned not to question them.

The landlady was something he hadn't counted on. He'd expected a comfortable, homey woman, with sensible shoes and sensible hair pulled back in a sensible bun. Instead, he had found Amanda Clayson.

She was sweet innocence all wrapped up in sun-dried cotton and mountain-fresh air. With her gold-tipped hair and chocolate-colored eyes, she looked like a particularly delectable angel.

He was trained to notice physical details. Like the tiny heart-shaped birthmark on her elbow. And the way her hair held a hundred different shades, ranging from the palest gold to the richest auburn.

She used her hands when she talked, gesturing with them in a manner that told Lucas it was habitual. When she was quiet, she clasped them in her lap, as though to hold them still.

Amanda and her boarders might be a little strange, but they were honest and unimpressed by his fame. He wasn't Lucas Reed, best-selling writer, but simply Lucas, another boarder who was expected to make his bed in the mornings and pick up after himself.

Fawning fans irritated him. And if he couldn't get some character studies out of this unconventional household, he wasn't the writer his publicist made him out to be. The writer in him was ever on alert—observing, evaluating, categorizing, just as he had when he'd been a cop. The two fit together better than many thought.

Dinner was a noisy, boisterous affair punctuated with laughter and occasional arguments. Lucas helped himself to the plentiful food, surprised to discover he wanted seconds. At his condo, he ate whatever he could find in the freezer, paying scant attention to what it was. Now he was enjoying Amanda's cooking as if he'd been on a starvation diet.

He dug into his second helping of meat loaf and mashed potatoes and watched the byplay at the table.

The others laughed together like friends, argued like family. He liked it. And them.

He had fans, but they weren't the same as family. He had good relationships with his agent, publicist, and editor, but even he wouldn't describe them as friends.

Lucas tried to determine how Amanda managed to make everyone feel that he or she was the most important person in the room. He had no doubt the others shared that feeling. Her smile poured over each of them, so full of warmth and light that he nearly basked in its glow.

Florence Wanlass glowed under Amanda's gentle questions about her years in Reno. Rudy Goldblume beamed his appreciation as she complimented him on his new tie.

The questions began then. First Florence, then Rudy.

Lucas knew he was being vetted. To see if he was worthy of Amanda's attention. He must have passed, for Florence smiled widely and slapped him on the back.

"Fresh meat," she said in her booming voice. "We've been too long on our own. Heard all our stories so often that they're coming out of our ears."

Lucas turned a tolerant smile on her. "Don't you mean fresh ears?"

She grinned at him before turning her attention on Amanda. "You promised we'd have a game of rummy," she said as Amanda cleared the table.

"I'm sure Lucas would be a much more worthy opponent," Amanda said with a glance his way. "Why not challenge him to a game?"

Florence fixed him with a speculative look. "How about it? You up to a game of cards?"

Lucas was about to refuse when he saw the eagerness in her eyes. He was trapped. He looked at Amanda, who sent him a wink. Neatly trapped by a beautiful chocoholic who gave him an innocent smile. "Sounds great."

Florence pulled a well-used deck of cards from a side table and dealt them out with surprising expertise. "I was a dealer in Reno before I married The Mister."

Two hours later, he discovered Florence Wanlass took her cards seriously.

"I win again," she crowed. She all but danced around the room before settling back in the chair to fix Lucas with a steely look. "One more game."

Lucas had spent five years in vice before transferring to homicide. He knew every con there was and then some. He could spot a cardsharp blindfolded. Florence Wanlass was cheating, but he'd be darned if he could find out how she was managing it.

He pushed his hair back from his forehead. He was playing cards with an eighty-something-year-old woman who he knew was cheating. What's more, he was enjoying it.

She lifted her gaze to his. The grin she flashed told him she knew he knew and didn't care one iota.

He couldn't help it; he grinned back. He was willing to bet Florence not only knew the ropes but had probably climbed a few in her day as well. His opinion of her ratcheted up another notch as she asked intelligent and incisive questions about his work on the force, all the while cheating him blind.

"Beat you five games out of five," she bragged. "Fair and square. Right?"

"Right," Lucas agreed. "Fair and square."

"I'll see what Rudy's up to," she said with another wink.

Appreciating her, Lucas gave a low whistle as she sashayed her way out of the room with a queenly bearing that no doubt had once captured the attention of men from eighteen to eighty. Florence Wanlass had some first-class moves.

He had been a cop for twelve years and was still looking for his first normal person. He had the unsettling feeling that he wasn't going to find one in this household.

A light from the porch drew him. The screen door was freckled with insects. Startled moths flitted and darted about when he opened it.

He found Amanda there. No sunlight spun its magic over her hair now. But moonbeams, he decided, worked their own kind of sorcery. A softer, subtler kind that suited her as well as the more brilliant light of the sun.

He took his time studying her. Her face was in repose now, a contrast to its usual animation. She rocked gently, swaying in rhythm to the motion of the swing.

She was singing something in an off-key voice.

He remained still, loath to intrude on the beauty he'd stumbled upon.

"Do you want to join me?" Her voice jolted him from his thoughts. She had known he was there the whole time.

"If I'm not disturbing you."

She patted the seat beside her. "The night belongs to anyone who needs it."

Her words kindled his curiosity. "How do you 'need' the night?"

A slight shrug lifted her shoulders. "The same way you need the sun." She placed a hand on her heart. "Here."

He settled in the swing, his weight disturbing the balance so that she slid toward him. His arms steadied her. "What do you find in the night?"

Moonbeams caught the slight tilt of her lips. "Peace. Harmony." Her smile deepened. "What do you find?"

Silence. For he had no answer.

"I don't know," he said at last, when he realized she had no intention of breaking the silence. "I never thought about it."

Without competition from city lights, the stars shone brightly. "They're beautiful," he said. Reluctantly.

"Stars are God's promises to us."

And he thought *he* was a writer. Amanda had a way with words that put his to shame. She was close, close enough that he could smell the chocolate. He wondered if she'd taste as sweet.

If he thought she'd supply the normal small talk, he was destined for disappointment.

"If you listen carefully, you can hear the fairies singing."

He started to smile, only to stop when he saw that she was serious. "Fairies?"

Her hair fell across her face as she nodded. "They come out only at night. When it's safe."

Lucas let the quiet of the night weave its way around them for five whole minutes this time.

"What do they do?" he asked, catching the strands of silk and tucking them behind her ear.

"Play hide-and-seek with the moon."

As he gazed at her vivid face and bright eyes, he had the feeling his life had taken a sudden and unexpected turn. What was he doing sitting on a porch swing having a conversation about fairies?

"Amanda . . ."

She put a finger to her lips.

The trilling of treble notes pierced the stillness of the night.

In spite of himself, he was shaken. "It's only the wind." He wished he sounded more sure of himself.

"Is it?"

Whatever he might have said was lost in the symphony that serenaded the night.

She shivered slightly. The thin mountain air had a bite to it this time of night. Automatically, he slid an arm around her shoulders, drawing her close.

Her scent enveloped him, seducing and disarming him at the same time. His attraction to his landlady was a complication he hadn't counted on.

She bothered him. She bothered him a lot, and he had no idea what to do about it.

She didn't say anything, seeming to understand his need for quiet. There was no tension in the silence. Only harmony. Never had he known a woman so totally comfortable with stillness. Most, he'd discovered, preferred the sound of their own voices. He didn't worry about offending her when he pulled into himself and let his thoughts drift.

"Thanks for playing cards with Florence. You made her night."

"She's quite a woman," Lucas said with total sincerity.

"She cheats."

"You know she cheats?" he asked, unable to keep the surprise from his voice.

"Of course I know," Amanda said with a complacency that surprised him. "We all do. But we don't let on."

"I enjoyed it." He spoke the words automatically. And was surprised to find they were true.

Lucas tapped his foot against the porch railing. The mountain air filled him with a restless energy. He inhaled deeply.

"It tastes good, doesn't it?"

It did. It never occurred to him before that air had a taste. But it did. Or at least it did when he was with Amanda.

"You like living here, don't you?"

"It's my home," she said simply.

"You didn't start out here." Out of habit he'd run a make on her. Finding out the who, what, and why of Amanda Clayson had been child's play.

A clerk at a classy San Francisco law firm, she had the right connections, the right family, the right fiancé.

She'd chucked it all to run a boardinghouse and bake decadent desserts.

She shook her head. "No. But you already knew that, didn't you?"

He nodded, curious if she were offended or angry that he'd checked her out.

She was neither. "I had a choice to make. I chose this." She gestured around her.

Even under the muted light of the moon, the beauty of her adopted home was evident.

Lucas looked more closely, noting the weathered barn, the house that needed a new coat of paint, the poor condition of the fences. "It must take a lot of work to keep up."

She nodded. "A lot of work and even more money. I spent my summers here." She paused, remembering the happy days with her great-aunt. "It's old, and something's always breaking down, but I'd never give it up."

"Do you get lonely?"

She laughed. "When would I get lonely?"

"What about men?"

"There's Mr. Goldblume."

"He's on the wrong side of eighty. Do you ever date?"

She shook her head. "Not very often. The town doesn't boast a surplus of single men." Her easy smile made him feel slightly foolish.

"I guess not."

"I've read your work," she said unexpectedly.

"Yeah?" The notion gave him a surge of pleasure.

She nodded. "You must have met all sorts of people when you were a cop."

He thought of the victims, the crooks, the poor, the wealthy. All had somehow found their way into his stories, even when he wasn't aware of it. Before he'd turned thirty, he'd thought he'd seen all there was to see.

Instead, he was constantly finding out there was more.

"What do you think of my books?" When she hesitated, he added, "Don't worry. I've got a thick skin."

"Your hero . . . ," she said reluctantly.

"Jake? What's wrong with him?"

"He's lost his humanity."

Lucas wasn't surprised. Jake Bodine was no white-hat hero. He was a hard-nosed cop with no illusions about the world. His work took him to the sewers of the city, where he dealt with the scum who made their homes there.

Much as Lucas had.

He shrugged. "He's a homicide detective. What do you expect? That he's going to go around handing out religious tracts?"

"It's not that."

"What?"

"You kill everyone off. Anytime Jake starts to care for someone, you get rid of her."

"Jake's a loner. He can't be tied down." The critics loved Jake, as did a good portion of the reading public. Why did he feel the need to defend his protagonist against her criticism?

Despite his brave words, he didn't like feeling defensive about his craft. It was an unfamiliar sensation.

"Why not?" she probed.

He didn't have an answer to that. Nor did he have an answer for why the words had dried up.

Writing had, quite literally, saved his life. He had grabbed on to it after leaving the force and, to his continuing amazement, had been good at it.

His first book had made it to the best-seller list. The next seven had assured him of a reputation as one of the day's top suspense writers. So why couldn't he put two consecutive sentences together now?

A fax of the first two chapters of his current work to his agent had resulted in a none-too-subtle suggestion that Lucas take some time off and "recharge his batteries."

Lucas understood publishing lingo enough to know that it meant what he was writing was garbage. He had known it before sending the draft. Still, he'd hoped. Prayed that it was enough.

If he didn't have his writing, he truly did have nothing.

Not for the first time he realized how closely Jake's life paralleled his own. Lucas also was a loner, living and working outside the rest of the pack.

That didn't mean he couldn't separate himself from his alter ego. He'd known writers who had lost the distinction between fiction and reality and lived in a kind of twilight. He didn't intend to become one of them.

At least Amanda hadn't gushed over his books as most women did, didn't ask the simpering questions, like where did he get his ideas and did he ever need help with the research for the love scenes. He supposed he ought to be grateful for that.

The fact that she hadn't gushed—had, in fact, criticized his work—was a novelty. He'd grown accustomed to the flood of praise and empty compliments, expected them as his due even as he was bored to tears by them.

For some reason, it nettled him. The one woman whose good opinion he would have valued had told him in no uncertain terms that she found his books lacking. Her bluntness had caught him by surprise, and his respect for her upped another notch.

She was still smiling, her eyes wide, a dimple winking at the corner of her mouth. He longed to take her in his arms and find out for himself if her lips tasted as soft as they looked.

"Lucas," she said, and he wondered how many times she'd said his name in an attempt to get his attention. "Why not?"

"I don't know," he said at last, unsure whether the words were in answer to Amanda's question or to his own.

"I'll leave you to think on it." She stood and went inside.

He sniffed and realized that she'd left her scent in the air. Lilac.

Amanda quickly grew accustomed to her new boarder's routine. He preferred solitude in the mornings. She didn't expect him to join the family at breakfast and left a plate warming for him in the oven.

When he wandered downstairs at half past ten or later, she poured him a cup of coffee and continued about her business. When he wanted to talk, he sought her out. When, as was more often the case, he wanted to be left alone, she was happy to oblige.

She'd made the mistake of knocking at his door to invite him to join the rest of the family for dinner one evening. He'd nearly bitten off her head. Afterward, he'd had the grace to apologize.

He was considerate enough about most things; he even put down the toilet seat. He had the distressing habit of feeding table scraps to Harry, but she couldn't very well fault him for it, as she did the same thing.

She learned that he worked all hours of the night, the faint clicking of computer keys audible when she passed his room on the way to her own. He wanted privacy and was willing to pay extra for it.

There were no pictures in his room of family or friends. No mail came for him; the clatter of his fax appeared to be the only communication he had with others.

She wondered if it made him happy, if anyone could be happy, or even content, being so alone in the world. Occasionally, she caught him looking at her with an intensity that filled her with longing and apprehension. Something dark and dangerous moved beneath the controlled surface he presented to the world. A moody writer wasn't exactly the perfect boarder, but his money spent the same. What's more, he'd given her three months' rent in advance. With a little creative budgeting, she could stretch it to cover the new bifocals Mr. Goldblume needed. Then there was the matter of replacing the hot-water heater.

She filled a vase with peonies from her garden, then stood back to admire her efforts. The small chores of making a home, the dusting and polishing, arranging flowers and gardening, cooking and baking, filled her with a quiet satisfaction.

She'd tried to explain her feelings to her family, to convince them that she was where she wanted to be, doing what she wanted to do. They treated her new life as a temporary aberration and acted as though she would return to the city—and her senses—within a short time. No matter that she'd spent a year here already.

When the phone rang, Amanda looked at the caller ID and felt a cowardly urge to ignore its summons. With a fatalistic shrug, she picked up the receiver and dutifully said, "Hello, Mother."

"Your sisters tell me you've taken in another boarder."

"That's right."

"I hope this one is at least able to pay rent."

Silently Amanda counted to ten. "All my boarders pay their rent." She crossed her fingers at the white lie.

Loretta Clayson made a *tsk*ing sound. "Why have you turned your back on everything I hold dear? Do you know how hard the women of my generation fought to have a fraction of the choices you enjoy? And then you throw it back in my face by choosing to go live in that shack your aunt left you."

The refrain was a familiar, if unpleasant, one.

Amanda didn't try to defend herself. Nor did she try to justify her choices. She let her mother rant, made the expected noises, and, with a promise to call soon, gently recradled the phone.

She loved her parents and her sisters but couldn't be like them. The irony of it was that her family really did love her. Amanda had no doubt of it. They just wished she was a little more ambitious, a little more talented, a little more like them.

Amanda had always been the black sheep of the family. Mandy the Misfit, her sisters had labeled her. She didn't blame them. She'd never fit in with her ambitious and talented family. Her two older sisters and her parents were all lawyers.

Determining that she could not be a lawyer like her parents and sisters, Amanda had chosen the next best thing and worked as a law clerk. The work had bored her, but she'd kept at it, unable to find a reason to leave. Her life had been one long series of decisions by default.

When she'd discovered that Stephen, her fiancé, had been seeing the newest junior partner, all the while having Amanda doing his research, she'd sent him a bill for two thousand dollars for her work. His hurt and outrage had been balm to her wounded vanity.

The knowledge that the man she'd agreed to marry had only been using her had sliced away at her confidence, her sense of self, her dignity. After a long, hard look at herself, she had decided her heart hadn't been hurt as much as her pride. She had accepted his pro-posal. Looking back, she wondered why.

The honest part of her knew and was shamed by it. She was a hypocrite. She'd said yes out of some kind of sick need to please her family. If she couldn't get a dream career for herself, at least she'd found a man who had.

Stephen had been a mistake from the beginning. His smile had been too easy, his chin too weak. In ret-rospect, he reminded her of a particularly oily used-car salesman.

In those moments that came in the long hours before dawn, she admitted that she had been in love with the idea of being in love. She had longed for a family of her own. Otherwise, she would have seen through a loser like Stephen right away.

If she sometimes yearned for something more, she didn't dwell on it. Not that there was time for it anyway. Occasionally, the longing for a child, for a family of her own, crept up on her. When she grew hungry to hold a baby to her heart, there were the babies at the hospital where she volunteered once a week. Her work there, especially in the preemie unit, filled the empty place in her heart that pined for a child.

She smiled, remembering the day Florence Wanlass showed up, with a large dog of indeterminate breed at her side. She'd confided that she was low on funds but high on life and introduced the dog as Harry, named after her first husband.

Mr. Goldblume arrived shortly afterward, referred by

a social worker when the retirement home where he'd lived for the last ten years closed its doors.

The whole arrangement worked out perfectly except for one thing—money. There was never enough of it. The old house wouldn't run on love alone. It continually needed repairs, and they came dear.

Florence flowed into the kitchen, face flushed and eyes dancing. "The writer's a genuine hunk."

"I hadn't noticed." Amanda felt her face heat at the outright lie. How could she have helped but notice? Lucas was strong-boned, long-legged, with shoulders as sturdy as the pines that studded the surrounding foot-hills.

Florence gave an exasperated look. "When are the two of you going to quit pretending you haven't been checking each other out?"

Amanda dropped a wooden spoon into the dark batter she was stirring. "I don't know what you mean." She finally got her tongue around the words. "Lucas is a boarder," she said primly. "He's here to write."

But because Florence was a friend, Amanda allowed herself a grin and a roll of the eyes.

"May I join you ladies?" Lucas' voice caused her to start. The smile he gave her was bland in the extreme. How much had he heard?

She was torn between feeling pleasure at his presence and annoyance at the interruption. He hadn't shaved, she noticed. The dark stubble only added to the appeal of his angular, hard-eyed face.

She couldn't work with him around, at least not with

her customary efficiency. Recipes she could put together in her sleep eluded her. She made stupid mistakes, and, most disturbing of all, his absence was nearly as distracting as his presence.

So where did that leave her? With a bowl full of flour and eggs and absolutely no idea of what she'd started to make. Since he'd arrived, such occurrences had become commonplace. Her problem, she reminded herself, not his.

Florence gave Amanda a knowing look before strolling out of the room.

Lucas waited until Florence had departed in a flurry of scarves and Shalimar. "She's quite a lady."

"Uh . . . Mrs. Wanlass . . . Florence . . ." Amanda made the mistake of meeting his gaze.

His eyes sparkled with mischief. *He'd heard,* she thought. *Everything.*

What was she supposed to say?

"Can I get something for you?" she asked.

"Coffee."

That she could do. She poured a cup and handed it to him.

He took his coffee to the table, sat, and squared one leg over the other. His fingers, long and blunt-tipped, curved around the mug with casual strength.

She snuck another glance at his face, noting the lingering amusement in his eyes.

Lucas knew that she knew. It would only invite further humiliation if she said anything about the unfortunate conversation. Then the absurdity of the situation caught up to her, and she started to chuckle. She laughed until tears rolled down her cheeks.

She wiped her eyes. "I'm sorry."

"Don't be. It's gratifying to know I'm considered a hunk."

"She'll expect us to name our first child after her." Amanda could have bitten off her tongue the moment the words were out.

Lucas didn't appear to notice her discomfort. "It's a good thing she's not forty years younger. I know when I'm outclassed." He stood and closed the small distance between them. "Do you think so?"

"What?"

"That I'm a hunk?"

The question didn't deserve an answer, and she didn't give one. Even if she'd wanted to, she couldn't have said a word. Her mouth went dry as she became aware of his every move, every sigh.

He was as close as a heartbeat. She resisted the urge to move away. She was a grown woman, after all. There was no reason she couldn't enjoy the company of an attractive man. A very attractive man, she added, mentally tracing the strong line of his jaw.

He was near enough that she could smell the minty scent of his toothpaste. She found herself staring at his throat, mesmerized by the strong pulse that beat there. Her heart bumped against her ribs at his nearness.

He tapped her on the chin. "Thanks for the coffee." He took his coffee and went back to his room, leaving Amanda to stare after him.

Amanda had been drawn to Lucas from the beginning. He wasn't like Stephen, the kind of man a woman could easily forget.

She threw out whatever it was she'd started to make, but for once her mind wasn't on chocolate. Thanks to Florence, it was on her very appealing boarder.

Chapter Three

The country quiet kept Lucas awake and, at the same time, made him think of the city. Of the comforting and constant hum of traffic, of the pace that ran in your blood so that you quickened your step to get to the next corner, beat the next light.

Places this close to nature made a person slow down. Once you slowed down, you lost your edge. He couldn't allow that to happen.

So he kept up the pace, if only in his mind. Thoughts spun, tumbled one over the other, raced, yet his writing was stalled.

Just as he was.

He'd tried working in his room but found the small space stifling and overly quiet. Writing was a solitary business, and he'd never minded his own company.

Until he'd met Amanda.

He slid his laptop inside its case and headed to the kitchen. Perhaps a change of place would stir his creative juices. He hadn't dared analyze why he'd chosen the room where he was most likely to find Amanda.

Though it was barely six in the morning, he found her already there.

She looked up from where she was mixing some-thing at the counter. "It's a little early for breakfast."

"Couldn't sleep. Mind if I work in here?"

"Not if you don't mind me clattering around."

She returned to her baking while he booted up his laptop and opened the file for his latest manuscript.

The urge to track her with his gaze was maddening. Unwillingly, he gave in. Her skin, a creamy white, was lightly sprinkled with freckles. At the moment, it sported a dusting of flour and a smudge of chocolate.

Harry wandered in at that moment.

Amanda stooped to wrap her arms around the mutt's neck and nuzzle him. In return, the dog licked her jaw.

Lucas watched the animal with a sensation very much like envy pervading his senses. Saliva pooled in his mouth at the way her hands glided over fur.

With a final pat on Harry's rump, she stood and turned to Lucas. "Everything all right?" she asked, startling him and nearly causing him to tip over in his chair.

"What . . . uh . . . sure. Fine." He had to look away, afraid she'd see more than he intended in his eyes.

"You looked like something was troubling you."

Only you. But he couldn't tell her that. He looked at the computer and remembered what he was supposed to be doing. "I was just working on a plot point."

The truth was, he hadn't written a single page that was

worth killing a tree. It made him wince in disgust as he reread his last pages.

"Would you like some juice?" she asked.

He was still trying to talk himself out of being jealous of a dog. "Uh, no thanks."

She poured herself a glass of juice. Her lips puckered slightly as she drank, drawing his attention to their fullness.

He could feel himself slipping, falling into the web she spun with such effortless grace. He looked into her thickly fringed eyes and felt the familiar tug. The ache in his jaw told him his teeth were clamped together in reaction to her appeal. It was becoming a familiar sensation.

He'd never known a woman who looked so good first thing in the morning. Her eyelashes, a deeper shade than her hair, needed no mascara to lengthen them. Her skin, rosy pink with the glow of exertion, was as smooth as a baby's. And her lips. Her lips were soft and inviting.

The tip of her tongue was tucked in the corner of her mouth. He stared in fascination. It seemed that the slightest little thing about her caught his attention. She knocked the breath out of him every time he caught a whiff of her scent, a mixture of lavender and sunshine and chocolate.

She'd bundled her hair on top of her head in an untidy knot. A few wisps fell to curl about her cheeks and neck. He had taken to wondering about how many pins he would have to remove to have it tumbling down into his hands.

She cocked her head, and that enchanting little dimple appeared at the corner of her mouth. One more thing to notice about her.

He shifted irritably.

"Is something wrong?" she asked.

"No. I was just enjoying the view."

Color stained her cheeks. She didn't respond with a flirtatious smile as some women might have. Instead, she frowned. "You're a funny kind of man."

"That's what my critics say."

She laughed, the sound as bright as her eyes.

Part of his reaction to her was simple, the response of a man to a beautiful woman. He understood that, could even, upon occasion, ignore it.

What he couldn't ignore was the growing suspicion that with Amanda, he was poised on the edge between chaos and order, exhilaration and boredom, darkness and light.

Being with her was both peaceful and exciting. The contradiction of feelings she aroused in him continued to amaze him. How was he supposed to concentrate on his writing when all he could think of was Amanda?

He needed to stop thinking about her and focus on why he was here.

His book.

That tactic took him full circle. Right back to Amanda. She had worked her way into his writing. Jake's latest love interest had taken on her characteristics. Gold-tipped hair, brown eyes, a ready smile.

On her hands and knees now, Amanda attacked the

inside of the refrigerator with a rag and scrub brush. The woman never stopped working. Occasionally, she'd rock back on her heels and wipe the sweat from her face with her shirttail.

After finishing the refrigerator, she turned her energy to the French doors, polishing the glass to a fine sheen. "That won't last long," she announced with a trace of humor in her voice. "Not with Harry pressing his nose against the glass."

As though on cue, Harry ambled over and plopped his front paws against the glass.

"See what I mean? He likes to watch the squirrels." She lowered her voice. "I think they know he's there and wait outside the door just to tease him."

Lucas couldn't help it. He burst out laughing.

Harry turned, as though to ask, "What's so funny?" Apparently tiring of watching the squirrels, the dog laid his head on Lucas' knee.

Lucas gave Harry an absent scratch behind the ears, at the same time rereading his last pages. With no regret, he deleted the six pages he'd managed to write and started over. To his surprise, the words came.

He went with them.

Thirty minutes later, he came up for air, startled to find that he'd written five pages. He read them and decided they might just do.

By seven thirty, the others joined them. Amanda served omelets and the muffins she'd just removed from the oven.

When he caught himself reaching for a second, he raised his head and found Amanda watching him.

A sheepish smile worked its way across his mouth. "These muffins are lethal. If I stay here long enough, my cholesterol will skyrocket. Not to mention my weight."

She returned his smile. "Thanks, I think. That was a compliment, right?"

"Right." Forgetting that they had an audience, he reached across the table, intending to brush back stray tendrils of hair that fell in her face.

A discreet cough from Rudy Goldblume reminded him that they weren't alone.

He'd been at Sweetbriar for two weeks. It had more than lived up to its reputation. The food was exquisite, the scenery breathtaking. Both outside and indoors.

The mountains wore their aeons of beauty with grace and dignity, but it was Amanda with her vibrant spirit who continued to captivate him.

She was a homemaker in the best sense of the word. Cleaning and cooking didn't make a home, though she did both. Caring did. He'd seen for himself how much she cared. About Florence and Rudy. And Harry. And him.

He thought of his condo, a charmless box that would never be called a home. Done in beige, black, and chrome, it was designed to reflect the sophisticated lifestyle of a man on his way up.

A humorless smile flickered across his face as he acknowledged that he spent as little time there as possible.

And so he was here. At Sweetbriar, with a landlady who had the face of an angel and the smile of a sorceress. And a heart big enough to make a family out of strangers.

He knew nothing about families and everything about being an outsider. It startled him to find that, for once, he wanted to be on the inside. With Amanda.

She hummed a tune he failed to recognize. That was another thing that enchanted him—her incredibly bad singing voice.

He read the message her T-shirt sported. I NEVER MET A CHOCOLATE I DIDN'T LIKE. "Is that true?" he asked and gestured toward her shirt.

"I'm afraid so." She grimaced. "That's why I have a stair stepper." She started to stand. "Got to stretch the kinks out."

He reached to help her, his hand grasping her by the elbow.

"Thank you." She brushed his cheek with her palm, a fleeting caress that befuddled his mind.

He'd been sitting too long. Stupid. He rubbed his leg, trying to ease the pain that was his constant companion. The spasm didn't lessen, and he gave an involuntary groan as the muscle in his calf pulsed in stabbing time with his heart.

Amanda's gaze settled on him with concern.

That concern terrified him. If she started in with the same nurturing she gave the other boarders, he'd be lost.

"Your leg's bothering you, isn't it?"

He managed a nod and then shrugged. "It'll pass."

She laid a hand on his arm, and, deep inside, he felt the shock of her touch.

He looked at her, disturbed by the compassion he saw in her eyes. His gaze lowered to the hand resting on his arm, the fingers unadorned by jewelry, the nails unpolished. It wasn't that he'd never felt a woman's hand on his arm before, but this was—well, different. As if to prove his point, his heart gave a fierce kick.

It shouldn't have moved him, but it did, this small gesture of comfort. She moved him, simply by being herself.

She grabbed his hand. "C'mon."

He thought of asking what she meant to do, but curiosity kept him silent.

In the front room, she pointed to the sofa. "I give a pretty mean massage."

He doubted she'd ever seen a body as mangled as his, but he rolled up his pant leg.

At his wince, she knelt to help him.

He stared at her bent head. Unfamiliar feelings welled up inside of him.

She didn't so much as blink, only gestured for him to lie down.

He closed his eyes as her hands probed his right calf. Her hands weren't particularly soft. Her palms were lightly callused, her fingers strong. She used both now to knead the muscles that had tightened up.

She skimmed over the ridges of scarring, the result of the surgeons' efforts to save his leg. The bullet had ripped arteries and torn ligaments. The doctors had done their best, but the scarring was extensive. *Repulsive,* one woman had called the scars that crisscrossed his leg in a half dozen places.

He wondered what Amanda would think of the scars.

He needn't have worried. She traced the worst of the scars on his leg with her fingers. In some indefinable way, he felt like he had been healed.

The admission shocked him.

He'd sensed something special about Amanda the first time he'd seen her. A goodness that could lay his ghosts to rest at last.

No. Every sensibility rebelled at the thought. He hadn't been able to keep his distance, though.

Her fingers moved along his leg, pausing at the spot where the pain centered. They tightened and dug deep. His first response was to scream in agony, but the almost-scream died as tight muscles slowly relaxed under her hands, turning to jelly.

He felt the pain loosen a little around the edges. Months of physical therapy had lessened it, but nothing could totally erase it. The doctors warned him that he'd never be completely free of it. Most days, he managed to ignore it. Some, like now, he just endured.

She continued rubbing, kneading, coaxing the pain to ease and, finally, disappear. Her fingers slid down his leg, gently soothing away every ounce of tension, working their magic.

"I'm sorry," he said, acutely conscious of how offensive the puckered skin must appear to her.

"Why?"

"That you had to see that."

She traced the scars, her touch infinitely gentle. "I see a beautiful man who has suffered more than he deserves."

Never had anyone looked beyond the ugliness to the man beneath. The physical wounds had healed, but the emotional ones remained. It took this woman to recognize that.

She hadn't been repelled by him, only moved by what he had suffered. The unspoken communication, this empathy, was one with which he had no experience. It unnerved him.

He had no armor against the understanding he saw in her eyes. Revulsion, disgust, he could have dealt with. And had. But the unwavering acceptance that Amanda gave was more powerful than any weapon he'd ever faced, more terrifying than any opponent.

"Don't you want to know how I got them?" He recalled a day at the beach six months ago. His date, whose name he couldn't even remember now, had shown a morbid curiosity about each and every scar. Her horror was only outstripped by her delight in the details.

"Only if you want to tell me."

Oddly enough, he did. Her gentle gaze was more effective than any interrogation he'd ever endured.

"I killed my partner." The bald words said too much and, then again, not nearly enough. When she didn't react, he kept talking, not censoring his words, not giving himself time to think. "I was a cop for twelve years. But

I got cocky, arrogant. Because of me, my best friend left a widow and a kid behind."

She didn't recoil, only took his hand and pressed it between her own smaller ones. "Tell me."

"A snitch told us that someone in the department was on the take. We narrowed it down to two detectives in our division and decided to follow them. The first was clean, so we turned our attention to the second. He must have gotten wind that we were on his tail, because he was waiting for us, weapon drawn. Danny saw him first—told me he was going to draw his fire.

"I was supposed to cover him, but my gun jammed. Stupid thing refused to fire." His voice grew harsh in memory. "Danny died because I didn't cover him. He counted on me, and I let him down."

"And you think it's your fault?" Amanda said. "That your gun jammed?" She didn't give him time to answer. "Tell me. Did you check it before you went out?"

"Of course, but—"

"Did it work then?"

"Yeah. But I should have—"

"What? Should have predicted that it would choose that moment to fail?"

"You've got it all wrong. I was the senior partner. Danny had just earned his detective's badge. I should have been the one to draw fire. Instead, my partner took a bullet."

He spit out one succinct word at the memory. "I went to the department shrink. I can live with Danny's dying. You don't become a cop without knowing the score."

Pain dug a little deeper. Maybe the shrink was right. He had survivor guilt because, no matter how he looked at it, Danny had been the better person, and he, Lucas, would have to spend the rest of his life remembering that.

It should have been me.

"Then what is it?"

"I can't live with profiting from it."

He saw the flash of understanding in her eyes. "*Substitute in Death,*" she said, naming his first book.

The hero, Jake Bodine, had escaped death only to see his partner die in his place.

"Got it in one." His mouth twisted in a parody of a smile. "I get a bullet in the leg and an early pension. Then I write a couple of books and make hundreds of thousands of dollars. All I had to do was sell my soul." The knowledge was a tight pain in his gut, and that pain was the dark thing that drove his writing. Now he didn't even have that.

"Was it your fault that your gun jammed?"

"That's not the point."

"It's exactly the point. Did you force Danny to take the assignment?"

Lucas made a rude noise.

"So you lived and he died. What if it had been the other way around? What if Danny had lived and you'd died? Would you want him beating himself up over it every day for the rest of his life?"

"Of course not . . ." It shouldn't be that easy. Couldn't

be. He tried to find a way around her logic. "You've got it all wrong," he said at last, but he couldn't figure out just how she was wrong.

"Do I?"

"I'm getting stinking rich, and Danny's gone. It should have been me."

Guilt was a ruthless master. He'd replayed the scene over and over in his mind, wondering what he could have done differently. His last picture of his partner was Danny drawing fire, certain that Lucas was covering him. The memory of it had ice rolling through his gut.

"We can't always comfort ourselves with blame."

"Is that what you think I'm doing?" Masculine outrage rimmed his tone. "Comforting myself?"

"It's easier to blame yourself than to admit that there was nothing you could have done to save Danny. It's a kind of arrogance to think you could have prevented what happened, to assume responsibility for what you couldn't control."

"He depended on me to back him up. It's my fault."

"Danny was there because he chose to be," Amanda said. "In the end, we're all responsible for ourselves."

He'd told her about his past, his failures, in an attempt to point out the differences between them. And, he admitted, to warn her away. Instead she was defending him.

He didn't deserve such generosity of spirit. He, who had failed his partner, didn't deserve the understanding she gave so effortlessly.

Amanda wasn't the first to try to talk him out of his guilt. After it had happened, friends had tried to remind him of all the criminals he'd put behind bars, of how many lives he'd saved during his years on the force. Nothing they said, though, could undo what had been done.

The department shrink had taken a turn. Her words didn't make a dent in the guilt Lucas heaped upon himself. He couldn't make atonement because nothing would bring Danny back.

It didn't matter that he'd failed for reasons not under his control. It didn't matter that, according to others' definitions, he hadn't failed. Danny was dead. How could that be anything but a failure?

Amanda's understanding didn't make sense.

But it didn't have to. Because his reaction wasn't logical.

It was sheer, raw emotion.

Every time he thought of Danny, he had to confront the pain of that devastating night in the alley.

Amanda read the rejection in his eyes and sighed. She'd made him angry. He'd expected sympathy, perhaps a few tears on her part. She'd challenged those feelings. She hadn't given him what he was accustomed to, and now he didn't know how to react, except to push her away.

Whether she was right or not didn't matter. It only mattered what Lucas thought, what he felt. And, according to him, he was to blame for his partner's death.

She noticed that her hands had started to tremble, whether in need to give comfort or to receive it, she wasn't sure. She tried once more. "Would Danny want you to spend the rest of your life blaming yourself for what wasn't your fault?"

"No." His harsh tone was all the harsher because he didn't raise his voice.

She skimmed a finger down his arm. He stiffened, and she could all but feel the pain pulse through him. "Then why are you?"

The glare he directed her way was rueful. "You're ticking me off so that I'll stop feeling sorry for myself."

"Looks like it worked."

"All right." His eyes closed. "All right. Supposing you're right, that doesn't let me off the hook."

"No, it doesn't. It doesn't let you off the hook of living, of doing what you were meant to do."

"Guilt's a greedy son of a gun," he said. "It needs to be fed on a regular basis, or it eventually dies. I don't want it to fade. I want to be able to remember. I have to remember."

She had an idea of what this sharing of his private thoughts and feelings was costing Lucas. His bleak expression warned her to be very careful of her next words. Intuitively she knew that offering the platitude, however true, that his partner's death wasn't his fault would only push him away.

Nothing she could say would ease Lucas' guilt. Not until he decided to let it go. Until then, he would continue to scourge himself.

She gave in to the need to touch him and laid her hand on his cheek, telling him with her touch what she knew he would reject in words. She sensed that this betrayal of need was alien to him.

Her heart contracted as she watched the shutter come over his eyes.

"Let it go," she said at last. "You've suffered enough."

Lucas knew he hadn't begun to pay his debt.

Amanda saw a knight in shining armor in his battered body. He couldn't even walk without a limp, but she didn't seem to notice.

Her sweetness, her goodness, were weapons against which he had no defense. They cut through his pain, right to the core. He had been a homicide cop, had seen more than Amanda could ever guess, yet he was powerless against the gentle understanding in her eyes.

He tapped his leg. "This is as good as it's going to get. The doctors did everything they could. For a while they thought I might lose it."

She didn't recoil from the idea but only brushed her hand down his jaw.

The palm she fitted to his cheek felt so good, so right that he resisted questioning the gesture, resisted pulling away. He flattened his hand over hers. That didn't mean he accepted her version of the truth, though.

"Why can't you see what everyone else does?" he asked, bitterness layering the words. "A burned-out cop. A lousy writer." The words were ripped from him. He didn't bother trying to hide the pain or self-pity behind them. He'd already learned that Amanda could see past any of his feeble attempts to conceal his feelings.

Amanda had a way of listening that made her hear the meaning behind his words. He waited, certain she'd have a list of ideas for him to put into practice, and was surprised when she had only a single question.

"Why can't you see yourself as I do?" she countered.

"Is it your job to look for the good in everybody?"

"No. Only the ones who deserve it."

He didn't have an answer to that. He was beginning to believe that he didn't have any answers at all when it came to Amanda.

She looked at him as though she really saw him, as if her soft brown eyes invaded areas others couldn't see.

Lucas rubbed his palm against his cheek, trying to wipe away the warmth left by Amanda's touch. Instead, the action only served to remind him of the tenderness of her hand.

He had no defense against the simple goodness of this woman. Maybe it was her smile. Maybe it was the way she didn't push. He wasn't sure what it was about her, but he ended up telling her things. About himself. About his life. About his feelings.

It stunned him, his willingness to confide the details of his past to her. It was as foreign to him as his physical response to Amanda, and he didn't like either. He had seen things no human being should have to witness. Along with his ideals, he feared he'd lost his soul somewhere along the way.

"What made you become a cop?" she asked.

The question took him back to when he was eighteen, eager and idealistic. "I joined the force fresh out of high school—went to the academy determined to be the best rookie there ever was. Thought I was going to wipe out the corruption, protect the innocent." He gave a self-deprecatory laugh. "I found out you can change some things. It's people you can't change."

She laid her hand on his. Intuitively, she knew that his physical pain was nothing compared to the loss of his partner.

"There was so much Danny and I wanted to do. We had plans. Big plans. We were going to clean up the department, then the city. We'd talk during stakeouts and dream of how it was going to be. Danny wanted a better world for his son, for other kids. Me, I just wanted to make a difference."

She listened. He wouldn't appreciate her tears, so she kept them to herself. She also knew he was leaving out much of the story, out of consideration for her.

"Danny didn't die right away. He knew he wasn't going to make it, but he smiled. Told me to suck it up. Then he asked me to take care of his family." Lucas swallowed, drawing her attention to the convulsive movement in his throat. "He died before I could promise him."

She wanted to touch him, to comfort him, but she knew better than to offer anything that smacked of sympathy. Lucas had erected so many barriers that she sometimes despaired of breaching them. But she would, she promised herself. One at a time, she'd bring them down.

"And did you? Take care of them?" she asked.

"I send money. Visit when I can." He shrugged it away. "It's not enough. It can never be enough."

Lucas had shaved his story down to the barest of details. Which only made her long to know more. It was both infuriating and endearing.

She was accustomed to so-called enlightened men who, once they'd learned it was all right to share their feelings, never stopped sharing. And sharing and sharing and sharing. Stephen had always been sharing—his feelings, his fears, his worries. Sometimes she'd wondered if she was his therapist or his fiancée.

"Lucas . . ." She knew he'd never crossed the line. He was a complex man, harsh, even, when it came to dealing with those who hurt the innocents of the world. And he judged himself with that same harshness. He didn't know his own goodness. Or if he did, couldn't accept it.

Not for the first time, she wished he could see himself as she did. He reached out to feather his fingers through her hair, sending warm, tingling feelings through her. She lifted her gaze to meet his calm, steady eyes and was amazed once again at the strength she read there.

He laughed mirthlessly. "Not much of a bargain, am I? An over-the-hill cop with more scars than medals."

He wanted to yank back the words as soon as he'd said them. He didn't want pity, he thought with a flare of anger. Least of all from her. His anger died as abruptly as it had flared to life. Amanda had too much pride of her own to feel pity for someone else.

"What I see is a man who believes in justice and fights for it."

He was tempted, sorely tempted, to accept the understanding he saw in her eyes, but pride kept him from responding to it.

"I'm sorry," she murmured.

"For what?"

She cupped his cheek, her soft palm fitting itself to the rough stubble. "Making you remember."

He curled a knuckle under her chin, tilted her face to his, and rubbed his lips over hers, a prelude of what was to come.

When the kiss came, she was ready. Or so she thought.

The kiss was a mere brush of lips. It shouldn't have affected her as it did. It stole the air from her lungs and had her heart doing flip-flops. Yes, it had affected her, and with an effortlessness that told her she was in trouble.

Big trouble.

She'd known a man's kisses before. So why did this one—this man—leave her so shaken? Tenderness, as sweet as the lips that had touched hers, unfurled within her at the gentleness with which he took her mouth.

She was safe, she told herself. Stars didn't explode inside her head. Not yet. Still, she hadn't expected the jolt, that hard bump of feeling.

His mouth was hard, his lips firm. But when they moved over hers, she felt herself melting. Into them.

The world had stopped, save for this moment, this

man. All that she could think of was what he was doing to her. And how he made her feel.

He made her feel just wonderful.

She gave and, in giving, received. He flooded her senses. Tastes, textures, scents. Each was sharper, tarter because of him.

And then there were stars. Bright, glittering stars that touched something deep inside her. It was every woman's dream. More, it was her dream.

At first she'd thought it was simple attraction, and there was plenty of attraction floating around between them. But that theory hadn't lasted beyond the first night when she'd talked him into playing rummy with Florence. He'd shown an unexpected patience and a genuine liking for her.

Stephen would never have taken the time to indulge Florence. It wouldn't have fit his image of the up-and-coming young lawyer. And Stephen had been very conscious of his image.

There she went again, comparing Lucas to her ex-fiancé. She had no reason to cast Lucas as anything but what he was. A boarder.

The idea that she might be thinking of him as something else, as someone else, someone who might occupy a permanent place in her life, was ridiculous.

That's right, girl. You just go right on telling yourself that.

From the moment he'd burst into her kitchen, he'd crowded everyone else from her mind. No wonder. He was everything a woman could want . . . and she was powerless to resist him.

She put a finger to her lips, not surprised to find they were trembling.

She wasn't supposed to moon over a simple kiss, she told herself. Wasn't supposed to yearn over it. Most especially she wasn't supposed to ache over it.

Chapter Four

Amanda couldn't rid herself of the memory of the bleak expression in Lucas' eyes. With her spirits already low, she looked at the letter that had arrived special delivery from the bank. When she summoned her courage to open it, she wanted to break down and bawl.

She'd been expecting the letter. Or perhaps a call. The county had granted extensions and was now demanding its money for the back taxes.

She welcomed the ringing of the phone. A distraction, she thought, from her problems.

"Ms. Clayton, this is Gerald Dodd."

Dodd was a real estate agent and had approached her when Aunt Roxy had died.

"How can I help you, Mr. Dodd?"

"I heard of your problems with the bank. I have an out-of-town client who's extremely interested in purchasing your property. He's willing to pay off the back taxes and give you forty thousand above market price."

Above market. "Why would anyone pay that much for Aunt Roxy's house?"

Mr. Dodd cleared his throat. "Well, it's not exactly the house he's interested in. It's the land."

She was beginning to understand. "What would happen to the house?"

"It would be razed to make room for condos." At her cry of protest, he added, "I know how you feel about the house, but a person in your position can't afford to be sentimental about what is essentially a pile of rubble."

"You've given me a lot to think about. How much time do I have?"

"I can't give you more than six weeks."

"Thank you, Mr. Dodd. I'll let you know."

For a moment, she was tempted. Forty thousand above market. That meant she could start over again. Somewhere else. And yet she knew she couldn't do it.

She could go to her family, ask them for a loan. Even as the thought formed, she rejected it. That would only convince them that Mandy the Misfit had failed at yet something else and would give them all the ammunition they needed to try to force her to return to the city.

She took a breath and felt a wave of hopelessness.

Her parents couldn't understand her commitment to keeping Aunt Roxy's home. It had been her refuge and her joy as a child.

It was in the old-fashioned kitchen that she'd learned to cook. Under Aunt Roxy's patient tutelage, Amanda had learned to sift, to measure, to stir. More, she'd learned to tend. Flowers. Vegetables. People.

She and Aunt Roxy had spent long hours in the garden, where they studied plants, bugs, dirt, but it hadn't been like a lesson, some sneaky educational ploy of an adult to a child.

No, they had crouched down and looked for the sheer pleasure of it. Had laughed when what appeared to be a speck of dirt scurried away on tiny legs. Little worlds, her great-aunt had called their subjects of study.

"Come," she'd say, "and let's see what we can discover today."

There'd been no lectures about wasting time, no reprimands about getting one's hands and clothes dirty. There'd been simple and uncomplicated joy.

Amanda swiped at an errant tear. Aunt Roxy had given her the gift of being a child. Nothing could have been more precious, nothing more needed by an awkward child who couldn't find a place in her very proper family. And the house, the rambling Victorian that had more leaks than a sieve, had played a large part in that.

The old house had offered shelter, and so much more. It had survived years and storms, the ruthless cold of winter, the sudden heat of high summer. Now, Amanda thought with a frisson of fear, it faced a different kind of challenge, one she didn't know she was up to meeting.

If she refused Dodd's offer and failed to find a way to pay the back taxes, she would lose the house to the bank anyway. The bank would have no choice but to sell it.

She pictured the house torn down, the beautiful orchards bulldozed so that the property could be turned into condominiums. Cold, boxy, and soulless.

The thought caused her to shudder.

No, her family would not understand. Nor would they understand her love for her two elderly boarders. Florence and Rudy had quickly become more than boarders. They were her friends and, in a very real sense, her family. She couldn't uproot them.

The house was filled with the homey fragrances of freshly baked bread, chicken soup, and, of course, chocolate, as well as a faint scent of lemon furniture polish, just as it had been when Aunt Roxy was alive. But now there was an energy in the air that had been missing before, as if the house had come to life.

Amanda knew it was more than the people who lived there. It was the love she and the others shared for one another. Caring for Florence and Rudy gave her purpose, the knowledge that she was needed, that she was making a difference. Her fiancé had taken that from her, had stripped her of any confidence that she mattered in a personal sense.

She understood that her parents and sisters wanted only the best for her. The trouble was, their idea of what was best was 180 degrees opposite of her own.

No, she wouldn't be running to her family and asking for help. She'd stand or fall on her own. Either way, it would be her doing, her choice.

"What's got you looking like you haven't got a pot to cry in?" Florence wandered into the kitchen just as Amanda placed the phone in its cradle.

Despite her worry, Amanda grinned. Trust Florence to say just the right thing. She thought about keeping her worry to herself, then changed her mind. Florence was part of her family.

"Money. I might lose the house." She hadn't realized how devastating the prospect was until she said the words aloud. Losing the house would be like losing Aunt Roxy all over again.

For a moment, Florence looked every one of her eighty years. Then she rallied and smiled. "I'm not worried. You'll think of something."

Amanda knew her friend was forcing a smile for her sake and loved Florence all the more for it. It warmed her. It also worried her, for it brought home that it wasn't just her own welfare that was at stake.

She reviewed her options. She could take a job in town. Be a clerk at a store. A secretary. Each held little appeal.

She would find a way. Somehow.

In the meantime, she had a family to look after. She gave her friend a smile she hoped wasn't too forced and did what she always did when life got too complicated.

She baked.

As she measured and stirred, she felt a pang of urgency. She had to find a way to keep the house. Making a home in Aunt Roxy's house was the only thing she wanted to do, the only place she felt whole.

Unashamedly, Lucas eavesdropped on Amanda's conversation with Florence. He waited until the older woman had gone to find Rudy before joining Amanda in the kitchen and slipping his arms around her waist.

She leaned her head against his chest.

"I decided we could use some cookies." Her voice lacked its customary lilt. Her shoulders drooped; her normally fluid movements jerked with tension and fatigue.

It was nearly unbearable to see her that way—Amanda, normally so filled with energy and love for life, looking so vulnerable, defeated.

He wanted to erase that look, to fill her eyes with the hope and light he'd come to expect there.

He waited.

When she said nothing, he began to grow impatient. Why didn't she tell him? Didn't she feel he had a right to know? The question startled him. Since when had he started thinking in terms of rights? They had no claim on each other.

Still, it hurt that she felt she couldn't confide in him.

He made a low, frustrated sound. What was he complaining about? He had no intention of sticking around any longer than it took to finish his book. The way it was going, he could be out of here within the month, a couple of weeks ahead of schedule.

So why was he fishing for reasons to stay?

Enough was enough. He put his hands on her shoulders and gently turned her to face him. "I heard you talking with Florence."

"You were listening." But the accusation lacked heat. Instead, she sounded relieved.

"Yeah."

The story spilled out. Back taxes. Bank threatening to foreclose. It sounded like a melodrama, only it was very, very real. And somewhere in the telling, she ended up in his arms.

"What am I going to do? I can go somewhere else, find a job, but what about Florence and Rudy?"

Of course her first concern would be for the others, he thought. "You're something special."

"Mmm?"

"You really love them, don't you?"

She looked surprised he'd had to ask. "Yes. I do." The eyes she lifted to his were soft and defenseless.

She was still in his arms, where she felt small and delicate. Slowly, he lifted his head. Cupping her shoulders, he set her back only enough that he could see her face. What he saw there caused the breath to hitch in his chest, but he refused to give a name to it.

He could easily give her the money she needed. The temptation was strong to do exactly that. He also knew his offer would be rejected. Sweetly but firmly rejected.

He'd have to find another way to help her.

"Thank you." Her husky voice did things to his insides that had nothing to do with the current problem.

"For what?"

"For not offering to give me the money." She touched his cheek. "I know you wanted to."

His nod was rueful. She knew him, what's more, understood him. The realization was a sobering one.

"My family would be gratified to learn that I'm finally

suffering for my lack of ambition." She smiled wryly. "You don't happen to have a spare miracle in your pocket, do you?"

He couldn't return her smile even though he knew she was expecting it. "Sorry, I'm fresh out of miracles."

She leaned her head into his chest. "What am I going to do?"

"I've done some accounting when I was in white-collar crimes," he said. "Maybe I could look at your books, come up with something."

The gratitude in her eyes had him hoping he could make good on his words.

"We'll figure something out." They stood there, rocking together.

Now, where had that come from? Hadn't he decided that he needed to finish up and get out of here before he did something stupid? Right now he wasn't prepared to define *stupid*.

Though everyone tried to be upbeat during dinner, the effort fell flat. It was with relief that Rudy and Florence retired. Lucas helped Amanda with cleaning up, then folded his arms around her, wrapping her in warmth and comfort.

Lucas kept to himself the next day.

The past had a way of hanging on, like a bad smell. He couldn't wash it away, no matter how hard he scrubbed. Even without the physical reminder of his leg, he would never forget that night Danny died, a night that had forever changed his life.

He'd left out the more gory details when he told Amanda about it, yet he sensed she had understood all he'd left unsaid, understood more than she should.

It had been over three years ago, yet he could recall every detail with horrifying clarity. The crack of gunfire. The smell of cordite. The gush of Danny's blood seeping through Lucas' fingers as he'd tried to stanch it.

He was losing ground where Amanda was concerned. The more he tried to rationalize his feelings, the tougher it became. He couldn't have said why the soft compassion in her eyes, the quiet understanding in her voice had made him nervous.

His resolution to forget the kiss they'd shared was impossible. Now wasn't the time to dwell on Amanda's charm.

He turned on the computer and started to write, but the words failed to come. His thoughts were centered on a beautiful witch who tempted him to want to live in the light after years of hiding in the darkness.

Chapter Five

The following day Florence hurried into the kitchen and grabbed his arm. "Amanda wants you."

"Where're we going?" he asked as he followed her outside.

"The barn. Peaches is having her baby. Hurry!" The beringed hand tugged more insistently until Lucas had no choice but to follow.

"Who's Peaches?"

She threw him an impatient look. "Our cow."

"Peaches is a cow?" He was going to see a cow give birth? Impatience flickered through him. One look at her expectant face, though, and he gave in. "Okay. Let's go see Peaches."

The sharp, pungent odors of hay and animals assailed his nostrils as he and Florence entered the barn. It took a moment to adjust his eyes to the dimness.

"Lucas, Florence, over here."

He followed Amanda's voice until he found her kneeling beside a cow. Random shafts of sunlight sifting through the rafters spun a golden haze over her hair, and he blinked against the effect. He took another look and realized that Amanda had her arm halfway up the cow.

She winced, and he guessed that Peaches had just had a contraction.

"It's all right," Amanda crooned. "Good girl. We're almost there. One more push."

Instinctively, Lucas knelt beside her.

"Hold her head," she directed, motioning him in front of her.

"But—"

"Stroke her behind the ears."

Amanda threw him an exasperated look when he hesitated. "There's nothing to be afraid of."

"I'm not—"

"Shh. I've got to give her a hand and turn it some. Just hold her head and talk to her softly." She spared him a quick smile before buckling down to the task at hand.

Talk to a cow? What did you say to a cow who was about to give birth? "Don't worry, Peaches. Giving birth is a perfectly natural process. Women . . . uh . . . cows have been doing it for centuries." *Uh-uh, Lucas. You're losing it. The lady tells you to talk to a cow, and you're doing it. Definitely over the edge. Too much sunshine and mountain air.*

He needed to get back to the city with its smog and exhaust fumes. If the boys at the precinct could see him now, they'd be laughing their heads off.

Peaches mooed impatiently.

Lucas imagined she was protesting the inanities he

was murmuring to her. He didn't blame her. He'd delivered several babies during his years on the force. Not one had scared him half as much as watching a twelve-hundred-pound cow push out a calf.

He cleared his throat and tried again. "Uh . . . it's okay. Everything's going to be all right." He stroked her velvety head.

Peaches bawled, and Lucas found himself wanting to bawl right alongside her.

"That's it, Peaches," Amanda encouraged. "C'mon, girl. You can do it. Push."

Peaches bellowed soulfully before straining her pelvis one last time.

"You're doing great," Amanda praised.

"Thanks," Lucas said, before realizing she was talking to Peaches. He felt the flush that heated his face. "I mean—"

Peaches wailed plaintively.

He risked a glance toward Amanda and saw her guide a tiny hoof out of the birth canal.

"Just a little bit more," she coaxed. "We're almost there."

A final wail caused him to wince in sympathy for Peaches. "C'mon, Peaches, you can do it. Don't give up now." Embarrassed, he raised his gaze to meet Amanda's.

Only the sound of Peaches' steadying breathing broke the silence.

"It's a female," Amanda said. If she'd announced the arrival of a check for a million dollars, she couldn't have sounded happier.

He watched as she cleaned the membrane away from the nose.

"Oh, Lucas, Florence. Isn't she beautiful?"

"Beautiful," he said, his gaze still on Amanda.

Florence cleared her throat. "I think I'll leave the rest to the two of you." The smile she directed at Lucas told him she knew exactly what he was thinking. And wanting.

Lucas watched as Amanda checked out the small animal, something twisting in his heart at the picture she made. She didn't appear to care that she was smearing her clothes with blood and birth fluids. Her hands were coated with both. She seemed oblivious to it, intent on her task. Her expression was tender. A damp gaze muted the brightness of her eyes. Tears?

When she raised her head, her smile was pure delight. Her arms and clothes were coated with blood and mucus, but it was her eyes that held his attention. They shone with an inner light that mocked the feeble rays of the sun as it tried to pierce the shadowy dimness of the barn.

"Beautiful," he repeated, his voice hoarse with emotions he refused to name.

"Help me pat her down," she said and began gently rubbing the tiny animal with straw.

Awkwardly, Lucas imitated her actions, gingerly patting it with straw.

"Look, Peaches. You have a daughter." Amanda gently pushed the little animal forward.

Something warm wrapped itself around his heart as

he watched the little heifer wobble toward her mother on spindly legs. The part of him that softened would never be able to harden again.

Tentatively, Peaches began licking her offspring, then turned to Lucas to give him what he interpreted as a look of gratitude. It didn't seem strange to him that he was crediting Peaches with feelings.

The baby rooted around, finally settling down to sucking noisily while Peaches mooed her contentment. Once again, she turned her gaze to Lucas, inviting him, he imagined, to share her pride in her offspring.

The kiss he and Amanda had shared made a mockery of his attempt to ignore her effect on him. He didn't want to be anywhere near this woman who was fast getting under his skin. Yet here he was, sitting not two feet from her, her scent wrapping its way around him, holding him hostage with invisible strings.

Something was shifting inside him. A door he'd thought locked tight was edging open, and he wasn't sure how he felt about it.

Light and shadow played across her face. Her lips were slightly parted. The tension had been growing between them, building and shifting like a summer storm.

"What're you going to name her?" he asked.

Amanda didn't hesitate. "Truffles. You're going to be a beauty, just like your mama," she said, stroking the calf softly.

Lucas watched the rhythmic motion of her hand, wishing he were the recipient of her gentle ministrations. He thought of the feel of her hands as she'd massaged his leg.

He watched as Peaches gently encouraged her baby, nudging Truffles with her nose. Most animals knew what to do instinctively, he reflected, but some rejected their young.

Like people.

And others gave love as easily as they breathed. Like Amanda.

He thought of how she'd taken in Florence and Rudy. And him. The thought gave him pause. He wasn't one of her strays. He was here to write. The pep talk fell flat.

He stood, and Amanda came to stand next to him. It seemed natural to drape his arm over her shoulders, to tuck her at his side.

"Where did Peaches come from?" he asked as she washed up with a bucket of water and a bar of soap.

He followed her example, plunging his arms into ice-cold water. She handed him a rough towel to dry off with.

"Some neighbors had to leave the state. They couldn't take Peaches with them, so I inherited her."

Another one of her strays.

"Let's give mother and baby a chance to get acquainted," Amanda said and backed out of the stall.

Lucas followed her into the light and drew a sigh of relief. The stall had been too cramped, too cozy for the physical attraction that had crackled across the narrow space between them.

She perched on a fence rail, locking her legs around a lower rung. He propped a hand on either side of her.

"You were great back there," he said. "Do you do this often? Play midwife to cows?"

She shielded her eyes against the glare of the sun. "This was my first time."

"You handled it like a pro."

"Thanks. You weren't half bad yourself."

He shrugged. "I did what I was told. You and Peaches deserve all the credit."

She shook her head. "Peaches did the work. I was just her coach."

"You make a pretty good coach."

Rich color flooded her cheeks at the compliment. "Have you ever seen anything like it?" Her voice was breathless, her eyes brimming with tears, tears he longed to wipe away.

But he didn't touch her; he couldn't, not if he wanted to maintain the distance he'd decided was crucial whenever he was around Amanda. It didn't help that Amanda was the kind of vivacious, open woman who made him want to smile for no reason at all.

He'd never been much of a smiler.

She was sunlight and moonbeams.

He was night shadow.

She'd built her world upon believing the best of others; his was grounded in the harsh reality of life on the streets.

Lucas didn't know what to make of his feelings. They were completely different from any he had ever experienced. This wasn't the familiar sensation associated with simple physical attraction. It was more, much more. And as unsettling as the woman herself.

Her freckle-dusted nose and sunny hair made him

think of a slightly mischievous angel. He almost expected to see a lopsided halo perched atop her head.

He wanted to memorize this moment, to absorb the sounds and scents. Dust motes highlighted by the sun streaming through the high windows danced gleefully in the air.

"Seeing a new life come into the world has to be the most wonderful thing there is," she murmured.

"Wonderful," he echoed, his gaze once more resting on her. He'd known plenty of women, all of them talented, bright, and ambitious, each of them more beautiful than the last. But he'd never known a woman like Amanda.

She wore no exotic fragrances, and right now she smelled distinctly of barn and cow. Bits of straw still clung to her hair, her clothes were wrinkled and blood-stained, her face free of makeup and liberally streaked with dirt and God knew what else . . . She was the most beautiful woman he'd ever seen.

Funny, he'd never before appreciated how appealing an unpainted mouth could be. Touchable. Kissable. The women who normally buzzed in and out of his life were painted to the gills.

Doubt and uncertainty fled at the emotion he read in her eyes. He leaned closer, his lips a breath away from her skin.

She had the trick of keeping him off balance. He knew only one thing for sure: no matter what happened next in their relationship, he needed to make certain he had control over it.

He'd seen too much of the world's ugliness. How could he bring that to a woman who viewed the world with love and light?

It snarled his conscience into a tight knot.

He looked into her chocolate brown eyes and knew he was playing with fire. Women like Amanda wanted promises of happily ever after and all that went with that. He wasn't made for it. He didn't even believe in love, so how was he supposed to promise it?

Amanda was rarely what he expected her to be or wanted her to be. She was herself. And that spooked him.

Once again, she'd managed to surprise him. He wasn't certain he liked it. A cop stayed alive by pigeonholing people, predicting how they would react in any given situation. Amanda defied his attempts to fit her into a slot. Just when he thought he had her figured out, she did something to turn his theories upside down.

No doubt about it. Seducing her would be a fool's move. He'd never thought of himself as a fool.

"You don't like it, do you?" she asked.

"What?"

"Not being able to figure out where I belong." She didn't appear offended. On the contrary, she seemed amused. "Don't let it bother you. My family couldn't do it either."

He wasn't normally this transparent. In fact, he'd been accused more than once of having a poker face, but Amanda had no problem seeing into his thoughts.

And his heart.

Her voice dragged like velvet over him, warm and rich and comforting. He basked in it, let himself savor the feelings it engendered in him.

But Amanda was different.

Every instinct warned him that, with her, there could never be anything simple and uncomplicated. He kissed her anyway.

She let out a shaky breath when he lifted his head. "I guess that answers my question. What better time to kiss a man I like very much than after witnessing one of God's miracles?"

Miracles. The word brought him up short. Only children and fools believed in miracles. Or God.

She glanced his way and frowned. "You don't believe in miracles?"

"No." The word sounded as flat as he felt. For a moment, with Amanda in his arms, he'd almost forgotten. Forgotten his gimpy leg. Forgotten that, until a few days ago, he hadn't written a decent sentence in months. Forgotten that he'd killed his partner.

"If you don't believe in miracles, what do you believe in?"

"Reality. What I can see, touch, what I can accomplish with my brain . . . my hands."

"What about love?"

"What about it?" Disbelief roughened his voice.

"It's the ultimate reality."

He made a rude noise.

"Don't you believe in anything?"

"Reality," he repeated.

"You must be very lonely."

He started to deny it and then stopped himself. "What if I am?"

"I'm sorry."

"For me?"

She didn't say anything, but he read the answer in her eyes. It made him all the angrier.

"Well, don't be. I get along fine without any of your so-called miracles."

She didn't flinch at his tone or appear upset by his rejection of what she so obviously believed. "Don't sell them short. Miracles happen all the time . . . for those who believe."

He wouldn't argue with her. He couldn't, not when she so obviously believed what she said. But he pulled back. It was as much an emotional withdrawal as a physical one.

The sooner he was out of here, the better. He didn't need this kind of trouble. "I'd better get back to work. I'll see you later."

She gave him a look that was neither approval nor disapproval. It was as if she could see into his very soul. If he even had one. "Of course."

The even tone of her voice shouldn't have filled him with guilt.

"I'll check on Peaches before I go in." She headed back to the barn.

Lucas watched her, feeling as if he'd missed out on

something special. Irrationally, he was angry. Not at her, though he felt like directing his anger her way. No, his anger was all for himself. He groaned. He'd rather take a beating than see the hurt in her eyes.

Just as Eve had tempted Adam, Amanda had tempted him to believe. In miracles, in love. He wanted to be able to see the world through Amanda's eyes. And knew that he couldn't.

Who did she think she was to try to force him into believing in miracles? She might as well have asked him to believe in Santa Claus and the Easter Bunny.

He started back to the house, calling himself all sorts of a fool.

He ran into Rudy and snarled out a response when Rudy asked how Peaches and her baby were doing. The scenario was repeated with Florence.

"You're acting like the hind end of a mule," Florence said with her customary frankness.

Lucas couldn't deny the charge. Even more, he knew he was only making matters worse with his attitude. It wasn't as though he were hiding anything. He was in a rotten mood, and everyone knew it. What's more, everyone knew the reason why.

After checking on Peaches and her baby, Amanda attacked the barn floor with a coarse-bristled broom. Bits of straw and hay scattered; dust billowed around her in tiers, like the lace of an old-fashioned wedding dress.

Now, what had put that image into her mind?

The exercise strained her already tired muscles, but she kept at it. She needed the release of tension. Feelings churned together until she was quivering with need and want. Lucas had done that.

He was a complicated male package—rigid, edgy, brooding, guarding his thoughts and emotions with a fierceness that would put off most women. She had been on the receiving end of his bristly side, one designed, she had no doubt, to warn her off.

Too bad it wasn't going to work.

Why had he run from her?

And why did it matter so much?

She frowned. Everything had seemed fine. He had even relaxed the rigid control he kept on himself as they'd participated in the miracle of birth. Then, without warning, he'd withdrawn from her.

He'd rejected her just as he'd rejected every overture she'd made to get him to open up. The idea that Lucas might be afraid of her sent a frown skidding across her lips. The more she thought about it, the more convinced she became that she was right. It didn't excuse his hot-and-cold-running feelings, but it went a long way toward explaining them.

There were moments when she caught him staring at her with an almost wistful expression on his face, one that vanished the instant he realized she had noticed.

It was at those times that she realized how very much she was aware of him as a man. Oh, boy, was she aware. She kept telling herself it was just that caretaker's instinct of hers, that she could sense he was hurting deep inside and wanted to fix it as she had with Florence and Rudy.

The honest part of her admitted that it was more than that, a lot more, but her mind refused to deal with it.

She propped the broom against the stall door and surveyed the results of her efforts. The barn floor looked better than it had in months, but she was no nearer to finding the answers she longed for. Comforting ones. Ones that made sense of what she was feeling. Ones that didn't leave her doubting herself. Ones that didn't leave her wanting . . . needing.

Lucas Reed was an enigma. Warm and tender one moment, aloof and distant the next.

The memory of his kiss was still imprinted against her mouth. And her heart. The very thought caused a laugh to bubble up inside her. She was definitely punchy. So she did what she always did when her emotions went haywire.

After a shower, she went on a cooking binge that left every square inch of the kitchen covered in chocolate. She didn't care. She baked cakes, cookies, éclairs, each richer and darker than the last. What was worse, she sampled a good portion of them.

How could she go back to thinking of Lucas as only a boarder? Truth be told, she'd stopped thinking of him in those terms weeks ago. So where did that leave them?

She bit into an éclair. Her hips were not going to thank her for this afternoon's work. She could practically feel the cellulite puckering up to make room for more fat cells. She wondered how many women had eaten their way out of a wardrobe because of a man. With a promise to herself that she'd spend extra time on the stair stepper, she finished off the éclair.

By the time she saw Lucas again, it was evening, and she'd had time to put things into perspective.

He was an attractive—make that drop-dead gorgeous—man. It was only natural that she should be drawn to him.

She was proud of the way she managed to face Lucas over dinner, as if nothing had happened. And nothing had, she realized. Nothing that mattered, anyway.

She felt his gaze on her several times. She returned it with a bland one of her own.

Amanda didn't putter around in the kitchen after the cleaning up was done, as was her custom. He ought to be relieved, Lucas thought, as he booted up the computer.

His fingers paused over the keys. Were those her footsteps approaching the kitchen? The smile that was still more thought than fact died when he looked up to see Florence.

"Sorry to bother you," she said, opening the refrigerator door. "I'll just get my glass of milk and scoot out of your way." She puttered about, talking all the while as she heated the milk and then washed the cup and pan.

His concentration shot, he admitted he wasn't accomplishing anything and headed upstairs. He paused outside Amanda's room, hoping to hear something . . .

anything. Only an oppressive silence greeted him, and he made his way down the hallway to his room.

He was accustomed to not sleeping. To being tired. He was even accustomed to fighting his own memories.

What he wasn't accustomed to was losing that fight.

He wanted to blame his sleeplessness on the noises of the night—a cricket serenading his mate, the gentle swish of a breeze, Peaches' occasional lowing.

He hated knowing that it was a lie. Even more he hated admitting that he was losing the fight to a golden-haired witch with soft eyes and a tender heart.

With a savage jerk, he tossed back the covers and yanked on his clothes.

He'd blown it. Big-time. *Admit it, Reed, you're a loser when it comes to dealing with a woman like Amanda.* Maybe it was for the best. Hadn't he already decided she wasn't his kind of woman?

She was too soft, too giving, too wrapped up in the lives of others for a man like him. He didn't share easily.

He needed to find Amanda, to apologize. Maybe then he could sleep.

When he'd searched the house with no luck, he thought of the barn. He pushed open the kitchen door, startled momentarily by the brilliance of the stars. Accustomed to the suffocated starlight of the city, he was still awed by the splendor of a mountain night.

A faint light appeared through a barn window. He followed it. As he drew closer, he heard the murmur of a husky voice.

Her head close to Peaches', Amanda stroked the cow

behind the ears. The picture they made had a rush of sensation constricting his lungs.

Lucas strained to hear what she was saying.

"You're a proud mama, aren't you? You have a beautiful baby."

Peaches mooed softly.

A noisy suckling drowned out Amanda's voice.

Lucas stepped closer, the straw lining the floor crackling under his feet.

Amanda looked up. The quick smile that lit her face faded immediately.

He'd done that and knew a sharp pang of regret. "I thought you might be here."

"Couldn't sleep?" she asked mildly.

"No," he said, his voice as rough as the wood siding of the old barn.

"I wonder why." Her voice held only faint interest.

"You're going to make me say it, aren't you?"

She turned innocent eyes on him. "I'm just expressing curiosity."

"It's you. All right? It's you who kept me awake. Satisfied?"

She continued stroking Peaches' neck. "Maybe." Then she lifted her head to bestow a smile upon him.

And that quickly, he knew he was forgiven. He felt something inside him turn over with an unfamiliar, nearly painful lurch. Whatever pulled at his heart pulled hard.

He squatted down beside Amanda. "How's she doing?"

"Great. She's a real trouper, aren't you, girl?"

Peaches opened her eyes long enough to favor Lucas with a benevolent look.

"She likes you," Amanda said.

The warm feeling her words generated within him surprised him. Since when did a cow's approval cause a rush of pleasure?

His gaze rested on Amanda's profile. The muted light of the lantern bathed her silhouette with a soft glow made softer by the sweetness of her expression. She was more beautiful than ever.

She raised her head. "Is something wrong?"

Everything was wrong, he wanted to shout. He was sitting in a barn talking with a beautiful woman about a cow's welfare. A cow.

Some of what he was feeling must have been reflected in his face, for she smiled up at him. "Not your usual way of spending an evening, is it?"

"Not quite," he said with a laugh that had some nerves in it. "About this afternoon—"

He didn't know what he wanted to say. He only knew he was in over his head with this woman.

"Thank you for sharing this with me," he said as both their gazes fixed on the struggling calf.

"You're never what I expect you to be," she said.

He wasn't what he expected either. Not lately. Not since he'd come to Sweetbriar. Not since he'd met Amanda.

Chapter Six

Lucas had closeted himself in his room.

Maybe it was the mountain air. Maybe it was Amanda's heavenly cooking. Maybe it was a lot of things. Whatever it was, Lucas had his groove back. More precisely, he was writing.

Jake Bodine wasn't behaving predictably. An unexpected streak of vulnerability had reared its head, taking him into new channels, revealing new layers.

Lucas went with it. His protagonist had developed a mind of his own, ignoring the plot line of his creator. The excitement that had accompanied his first few books returned.

The love interest, up until now a vague figure in his books, assumed a more prominent role. Not surprisingly, she bore a striking resemblance to Amanda.

There were secrets beneath her apple-pie exterior. His heroine would discover hidden strengths as she was stalked by a madman. Lucas had a feeling she was going to become a permanent part of the cast.

He wrote as a man possessed, barely taking time to eat or to sleep. He resented having such basic needs and spared the minimum of time on both. As for anything or anyone else, they ceased to exist.

Amanda, bless her, left his meals outside his door. He didn't see her or the others for the next five days. He wrote until exhaustion and hunger forced him to stop.

When he surfaced long enough to look at his room, he winced. A glance at himself in the mirror elicited a string of curses that would do Jake Bodine proud. He looked—and smelled—like something that ought to be shot and put out of its misery.

But even that couldn't dim the satisfaction that settled over him like a comfortable sweater. He was writing again. What's more, it was good.

He felt it.

Freshly showered and shaved, he emerged from his room, hungry for food and, to his surprise, company. He sniffed once. Twice. The kitchen, redolent with the aroma of melted chocolate, beckoned.

He wasn't any too certain about his welcome. He'd ignored Amanda for days, his only response a growl when she came to tidy his room. Most women of his acquaintance would toss him out for that kind of treatment.

He found her at the stove, stirring something that smelled as delicious as she looked. A pretty apron, tied about her narrow waist, made her look more appealing than ever. She smelled of sun-dried sheets and fresh earth, a heady combination. The scent was intensely female, both elegant and practical.

Her smile was confirmation that she wasn't most women. She filled a cup with coffee and set it in front of him.

He was tempted to fall to his knees to worship her. Instead, he cupped his hands around the mug, content to savor the aroma. After gallons of cop-shop coffee, he could drink anything. And had. That didn't mean he couldn't appreciate the superior brew Amanda served. Hers was nectar.

"You're a woman in a million, Amanda Clayson."

She planted her hands on her hips. "After hibernating like a bear, you've decided to charm me now, is that it?"

"Can I?"

"I'd say you'd already done that." She gestured toward a basket of chocolate muffins. "Help yourself."

He bit into one and sighed. Rich with chocolate and nuts, it tasted like heaven.

A casual question about Florence and Rudy elicited the information that they had taken a trip to town. Toenails clicking on the wood floor, Harry ambled into the kitchen.

Amanda removed the pot from the stove and poured the mixture into a bowl. She dipped a spoon into the bowl and brought it to his lips. Pudding. The humble-sounding name didn't do justice to the scent of rich chocolate.

Lucas stooped and rubbed his leg. Instantly, she was on her knees, reaching for him. "Let me."

"Just because we've shared a few kisses doesn't mean I want you fussing over me," he said in a harsh voice, at odds with the tender tones of earlier.

Slowly, she stood. She didn't deserve that and let the hurt show in her eyes.

"Heck, I'm sorry. I didn't mean . . ." He shook his head. "You can't take care of the whole world."

Was there something more in his words than the surface meaning? His eyes were shadowed as they'd been when he first arrived at Sweetbriar. The shadows were still there, but she'd caught the occasional glimpse of light as well.

Was he trying to tell her that she couldn't take care of him? Care *for* him?

She knew that she couldn't erase the memories that haunted him, but she thought she had helped. She and Florence and Rudy.

"I don't want to take care of the world," she said, her voice soft and slow with realization. "Just the parts I care about." *Like you.*

She reached out, only to drop her hand as the mask slipped over his face. She'd come to recognize it in the weeks Lucas had been there.

"You care too much." The words came out in a low mutter, and she flinched from the anger she read in his eyes. "You're great with the over-eighty crowd, Amanda, but you're way off base with me. Better stick with what you know." Without a backward glance, he walked away.

In his room, Lucas massaged his leg and cursed himself. That had been close. Too close. He'd hurt Amanda and despised himself for it. He sighed heavily.

A noise at the door had him crossing the room and opening it, half hoping he'd find Amanda there. Harry looked up at him with soulful eyes in that crazy, lop-sided face. Absently, Lucas stooped to scratch the dog behind the ears.

"You ever have woman troubles?" he asked.

Harry yawned widely.

"Guess not, huh?"

With a grimace for his mangled leg, Lucas straightened.

Amanda put a hand to her cheek. It was warm where Lucas had touched her. She concentrated on that, because the rest of her was suddenly cold. So very cold. She wrapped her arms around herself to ward off the chill. Only the coldness came from the inside.

Lucas had pushed her away. Again. It was becoming a pattern. He'd allow himself to get so close and then pull back. Something bleak and heavy settled around her heart with depressing finality.

What kind of man could kiss her with such heart-wrenching tenderness, then simply walk away?

The sigh that trembled from her lips was more of a sob. She clamped her hand to her mouth, then looked up to find Florence watching her.

"What's up with you and the writer?"

Amanda willed back the threatening tears.

Florence gave Amanda a long look. "I'd say you've found your soul mate."

She'd found that and more, Amanda thought. "I'm acting like a teenager with her first crush."

"You're acting like a woman in love."

"Is it that obvious?" To her chagrin, Amanda discovered that her voice quavered.

"To another woman it is." Florence folded Amanda into her arms. "I knew it. The moment I laid eyes on him, I knew he was the one." Tears gleamed in her eyes. "I'm a silly old woman, but I know love when I see it." Impatiently, she swiped at her eyes.

Amanda wasn't surprised at her friend's perception.

"You become vulnerable to everything he's doing."

"Or not doing," Amanda added. Like telling her that he loved her. "He'll hurt me. He won't mean to, but it'll happen all the same."

To her surprise, Florence didn't try to talk her out of her fear. "You could end up getting hurt. Or you could be happy.

"Did I ever tell you about how I met The Mister?" Florence asked, with an abrupt change of subject.

Amanda knew Florence referred to her first husband as The Mister.

"I was a dealer in Reno. I was a looker in those days." She patted her hair. "This was red. No henna rinse for me back then. The Mister was a cop, walking a beat.

"Anyway, I'd had my eye on him for a couple of weeks, but he'd never give me the time of day." Florence paused. "He'd taken to coming into the casino during my shift. When he walked in, I was dealing from the bottom of the deck." She made a face. "Management's orders. He busted me."

"You mean he arrested you?"

"Right down to the handcuffs and reading me my rights."

"Let me get this straight. Your husband arrested you and hauled you off to jail?"

Florence gave a saucy smile. "He wasn't my husband then."

"What happened?"

"He bailed me out. Then asked me out the next day. This led to that, and that led to this, and two weeks later we were married." Her eyes grew dreamy. "In a little chapel with a preacher who looked like Bob Hope."

Amanda was beginning to wonder if she'd been had. Florence had been known to stretch the truth sometimes to make a story better.

"Are you sure—"

"You're wondering if I might be bending the truth a smidgen. Am I right?"

Reluctantly, Amanda nodded.

"I may exaggerate about some things, but never about The Mister and me." Florence's voice cracked on the last words. "We were together for almost fifty years."

Amanda felt her heart stumble at the emotion in her friend's voice. "Why are you telling me all this now?"

Florence just smiled. "Love doesn't always make sense. It just is. Like The Mister and me."

"How do I convince Lucas to give us a chance?"

"Listen to your heart. It won't lead you astray." She gave Amanda a shrewd look. "You're in love with him."

Amanda wanted to deny it but settled for the truth. "With all my heart." Hurt and fear rushed out along with the admission. "He's pushed me away. He doesn't want me."

"That boy doesn't know what he wants. That doesn't mean he doesn't love you."

"He doesn't believe in love."

Florence snorted. "Most men don't. Not even when it's right under their noses." Her voice gentled. "He needs you."

"How do you know?"

"His eyes were cold, dead, when he came here. Now they're alive."

"What can I do?"

"Be there for him when he's ready."

Amanda wanted to believe it was that simple. She wondered what it would feel like to hear Lucas say "I love you." As much as she longed to hear the words, she couldn't force them. They had to be freely given, not out of her need but his. Until Lucas could say "I love you" and mean it, there was no future for them.

Oh, he was attracted to her. She didn't doubt that, but physical attraction wasn't enough. Not for her. She needed his trust, his respect. Most of all, she needed his love.

For Lucas, love didn't exist.

Amanda tumbled into bed that night, more confused than ever.

Florence meant well, but she didn't understand just how unapproachable Lucas could be when he put up barriers around himself. He would always resist making himself vulnerable and admitting that he might need anyone.

Though he'd told her precious little about his childhood, she'd guessed that he'd had to learn early to depend on only himself. The woman brave enough to love him would either have to accept the defenses he'd built around his heart—or very likely break her own trying to breach them.

Her head cautioned her to run as far as she could as fast as she could, but her heart betrayed her. If this was to be all she had with Lucas, then she'd grasp it with both hands and be grateful for it.

She didn't believe that her love was enough to keep him here forever. Neither was she proud enough to deny herself whatever happiness she found with him. It would be enough.

It had to be.

Chapter Seven

Amanda brewed coffee. She normally had tea in the morning, but today she felt the need for an extra jolt of caffeine. She had an hour before the rest of the family generally made their way down to the kitchen, and she intended to enjoy the solitude.

She reveled in the clutter and clatter of people and things. She didn't mind any of it, not a bit. Still, she savored this slice of quiet. She needed time to think about what had happened between her and Lucas. Love, the kind of love between a man and a woman that bound them together forever, wasn't likely to be part of the future for herself and Lucas.

Which meant she'd be smart to ignore whatever it was she felt for him. She was honest enough to admit that she needed much more from him than the casual level of friendship where he seemed determined to keep them. Unfortunately, the one person she could have talked with to make sense of her feelings was also the same person she wanted to talk about. Lucas. The man had turned her world upside down. She wasn't naive enough to believe that loving was the same thing as being in love. Unless a miracle occurred, she feared Lucas would never be able to give more than a guarded portion of his heart.

He hadn't exactly said that, but the meaning was there. He didn't want a permanent relationship. She accepted that. If she'd gone and done something stupid, like fall in love with him, well, that was her problem. She was responsible for her feelings. No one else.

Lucas had more sides than a multifaceted diamond, she decided. Warm and giving one moment, cold and remote the next.

He deliberately kept her at arm's length, as if he were scared of letting her too close. Maybe if she found a way to sneak past all those defenses he'd erected, she might find the real Lucas Reed. The glimpses she'd managed to catch of him were enough to convince her the result would be worth the effort.

When he showed up, his blue eyes clouded with uncertainty, she knew she couldn't hold on to her hurt. He was vulnerable, though she knew he would reject the label.

Acting on impulse, she kissed him. When he lifted his head, he looked bemused. Good. His kisses had kept her off balance for the better part of a month. It was about time she returned the favor.

Dressed in pink shorts and a striped top, Amanda looked as fresh as a summer morning. Golden freckles danced enticingly along the curve of her shoulders whenever she moved. Lucas' mouth felt unaccountably dry. As though nothing had happened, she picked up a dishrag and started to wipe down the counters.

He had forgotten to breathe. When he did so now, he felt curiously light-headed. "We need to talk."

"I thought we did that yesterday," she said without looking up from her task.

"I was a jerk."

"You're right."

"That's all you're going to say?"

"What else is there?"

"I'm sorry." The admission surprised him. He'd lived his life by the motto *Never apologize, never explain.*

"Was that so hard?"

"Not as much as I thought it would be."

A small smile inched across her lips. "Congratulations."

"For what?"

"You're making progress, Reed."

He stared at her. It couldn't be that easy. He hadn't been exaggerating when he said he'd acted like a jerk yesterday. She ought to be yelling at him or crying. Or something.

Her smile grew, a real, honest-to-goodness smile that punched him in the heart. "How about some breakfast?"

He was about to protest that he wasn't hungry, when he realized that he was. "Only if you sit down and let me fix it."

She plopped down in a chair. "That's the best offer I've had in a week."

He was no whiz in the kitchen, but he could make a

fair omelet. Whistling softly, he set about the task, conscious all the while of Amanda watching him.

"You're pretty good at that," she said as he beat the eggs with a wire whisk.

"For a bachelor, you mean?"

"For anyone."

The simple words of praise sent warm color rushing into his cheeks. He knew enough about Amanda to know she never said anything she didn't mean.

He popped bread into the toaster, poured juice, and set the table. Over the meal, he wondered how many times anyone had waited on her. Not many, he guessed.

For the span of the meal, he forgot he was here to do a job. He forgot that Amanda came with more ties than a store-wrapped Christmas present. For a few stolen moments, they were just a man and a woman enjoying each other's company.

They made quick work of the cleanup.

She scraped her hair back from her face and twisted a rubber band around it. With her hair in a ponytail, she looked about twelve years old. She then jammed a straw hat onto her head and held out her hand. "C'mon. We're going to pick apples."

Pick apples? A mental picture of sharing the task with her was unexpectedly appealing. Images of the two of them lying in the cool grass under an apple tree filled his mind. He would kiss the apple juice from her lips, lick away the tart sweetness with his tongue.

Amanda always did the unexpected. It was one of the things he liked most about her.

The thought caused his brow to furrow. If he didn't know better, he'd think he was falling in love with her. But he was safe. As long as he remembered he didn't believe in love, he was all right. And he ignored the little lurch that his stomach gave.

"Why today?"

"Today's an apple-picking day. And a picnicking day."

"What's an apple-picking day?"

She dragged him to the kitchen door and threw it open. "Look. Feel."

He looked. And felt. The day sparkled. Sun shimmered off the tin roof of the barn. A breeze, no more than a puff of air, really, found its way through the open door. The heavy scent of flowers past their prime perfumed the air. The sun shone down, a shining bowl of yellow. A breeze stirred the grass and brought the smells of earth and waning summer.

She was right. The day was begging for a picnic. It was filled with the kind of magic he'd come to identify with Amanda. She pulled a wicker basket from a cabinet and began filling it with an assortment of food. "I thought we'd take the ham left over from last night." She looked up. "All right?"

"Great." But his mind wasn't on food. It was on the way her hips filled out her pink shorts as she bent over the basket. It was on the softness of her voice as she hummed in her off-key voice.

She hefted the picnic basket. When he made to take it from her, she stopped him. "I have something else for you to carry. In the barn."

He followed her outside and inhaled deeply, relishing the mountain breeze. Seduced by both the golden day and the appeal of spending time alone with Amanda, he wrapped his hand around her free one. They headed to the barn, where she spent a few moments nuzzling Peaches and Truffles before pointing to a splintered ladder.

He eyed it doubtfully. "You're not going to use that thing, are you?"

"Sure. Don't worry. We're not going far, and it's not heavy."

"That's not what I'm worrying about." But his words were lost as she whirled away and gathered up three bushel baskets. She stacked them together, fitting the picnic basket inside the top one.

"Come on," she called.

"What's the rush?" He tucked the ladder under his arm and started after her.

She spread her arms, the gesture encompassing the earth and sky. "I don't want to miss a minute."

She was right. The first hint of fall hugged the air and gilded the trees. Summer-dried grass crunched under his feet. A bluer-than-blue sky provided the perfect canopy for the sun-washed day.

Tucked in the hillside to the southwest of the house, the apple orchard hummed with the buzz of bees.

"Don't worry," Amanda said. "They won't bother us if we don't bother them." She pointed to a gnarled tree laden with fruit. "We'll start with this one."

He leaned the ladder against the tree, more alarmed than ever. The tree loomed over them. The ladder creaked ominously as he tested it. "You're kidding, right? You're not going up there."

She gave him a surprised look. "Why not?"

"It's not safe."

Her laugh wrapped its way around him, soft, sweet, and utterly seductive. "You're cute when you're being overprotective."

Cute? "I'll go."

"Don't be an idiot. You're too heavy. The ladder won't hold you."

She didn't say that he couldn't make the climb with his bum leg. He doubted she even thought of it. Because she was Amanda.

"I'll be perfectly safe," she said.

"Amanda, wait . . ." His words went unheeded as she scrambled up the ladder.

"Don't worry," she called down to him. "I've done this dozens of times."

Don't worry! He fumed. She was climbing an ancient ladder that might have been used by Noah.

He released the breath he hadn't known he was holding when she made it to the top.

"It's great up here!" she yelled. "You can see for miles."

"Get the apples, and get down!" he yelled back.

"Spoilsport."

He watched as she stretched out on a branch to better reach the fruit. Seconds ticked into minutes, and he grew more anxious with each moment that passed. Every time she shifted, his heart stopped. He had faced down armed perps, broken up domestic battles, and taken in hyped-up junkies. Now, seeing Amanda perched fifteen feet above the ground, he realized he had never known real fear.

She filled the cloth bag tied around her waist. "Coming down!" she hollered. The ladder teetered against the tree as she started to back down, and he gripped the sides of it.

"Haul yourself down here right now, or I'm coming up after you." It was an empty threat, and they both knew it.

Her sack bulging with fruit, she turned and gave a jaunty wave. His heart jumped to his throat when she swayed slightly. He was up two rungs before he realized she was nearly down. He settled his hands on her hips, lifting her down the rest of the way and turning her against his chest as he assured himself she was safe. "You ever do something like that again—"

She kissed him.

He forgot what he'd been about to say in the sweetness of her lips as they found his. Automatically, his hands came up to grasp her arms. Shaken, he rested his brow against hers.

She turned a smile on him. "Let's go find another tree."

He picked the next tree, ignoring Amanda's protest that it was too small. All he cared about was that it was low to the ground. Soon they had the baskets overflowing with fruit.

"Time for lunch," she announced.

In the shade of a tree, they spread an ancient patchwork quilt on the ground. They feasted on ham sandwiches and wedges of cheese, washing it down with homemade lemonade. Sunlight, its pattern dappled by the leaves, gilded her hair, turning it into a gleaming cap of fire. It lit up her face, highlighting the smattering of freckles across her nose and cheeks. Once more he thought of the differences between them—sunshine and shadow.

It was pure pleasure just watching her. She smelled as fresh as the mountain air. No perfume interfered with the soap-and-water scent of her. He longed to kiss each of the golden freckles.

She rubbed an apple against her sleeve and handed it to him. His tongue curled as tart juice slid over it. "It's good," he said between bites. Things had a way of tasting better, smelling better, feeling better, when he was with Amanda. For once, he didn't stop to analyze the feeling.

He accepted it.

"There's nothing better than a just-picked apple." An apple crunched under her teeth. And she grinned. "Unless it's chocolate."

"You do this often?"

"Only in the fall," she said, her eyes bright with laughter. The amusement in her eyes spilled over into her voice.

"You're laughing at me."

"Just a little," she admitted, her voice full of fun. "Fall's when apples are harvested."

"You caught me. I'm a city boy."

"But a quick learner."

In no hurry to get back, they relaxed in the cool shade.

She fits here, he thought, *with the sun and sky and the backdrop of mountains.* Where, he wondered, did he fit? He didn't worry about offending her when he pulled into himself and let his thoughts drift. He realized he was beginning to take such silences for granted.

The setting couldn't be more perfect. Above them, the thin, high clouds were turning rose against a turquoise sky. The distant mountains gave fresh meaning to the word *exalted*.

"I like the mountains this way," she said. "They look at peace."

He was no longer surprised at her uncanny ability to sense his thoughts. Nor did he question her observation on the mountains. No tourist-trite descriptions such as "majestic," "snow-capped," or "beautiful" for Amanda.

She saw peace.

Never had he known a woman so totally attuned to what he was feeling. Tenderly, almost reverently, he brushed her cheek with the pad of his thumb. He stretched out on the quilt and drew her down beside him. Leaves crackled beneath them.

He wanted to know more about this woman. "What brought you here?"

"Aunt Roxy."

She told him the story, and he laughed at her description of her great-aunt.

"I wish I'd had an Aunt Roxy."

"What about your parents?"

He twisted away from her. "I never knew them. Not really. My mother was a kid when she had me. She tried to take care of me, but she couldn't hack it. She dumped me at social services, and I bounced from one foster home to the next."

Her quick gasp had him wishing back the words. "Hey, I survived. The families who took me in were good people. They just didn't know what to make of a kid who'd rather use his fists than his brain. By the time I reached high school, I smartened up."

She touched her lips to his. "You were lonely."

The last thing he wanted was sympathy. "Don't go feeling sorry for me. I joined the force after I graduated. It became my family." He didn't want to talk about the past. Right now he was far more interested in the present.

To distract her, he took her hand and brought it to his lips, kissing the center of her palm. He shifted his hand to cup the nape of her neck, tilting her head back and bringing her face up. The breath shuddered from him as he felt her tremble in his arms. His lips found hers. Only a touch, he promised himself.

The kiss was like the lemonade, sweet with a tart aftertaste. He gazed at this woman who had brought him, and his writing, back to life. He had stopped trying to convince himself that his feelings for her were something that would burn white-hot for a while before dying down to cold ashes. But he didn't delude himself into believing there was a future for them. No two people could be more wrong for each other.

They wanted different things. It wasn't only that they looked at the world from different perspectives; they weren't even looking at the same world. Amanda looked at hers through rose-colored glasses. Lucas had thrown his glasses away a long time ago. Twelve years on the force had seen to that.

For Amanda, home and family came first. Lucas didn't fault her for that; he even admired it. But it wasn't for him.

As much as he enjoyed the undeniable joy of being with Amanda, he didn't believe in love. He wouldn't—couldn't—take advantage of her feelings for him. Though he didn't love her, he did care for her.

He'd never thought of relationships in those terms before, but then, he'd never known a woman like Amanda before. She was baffling, frustrating, and too generous for her own good. She was also beautiful, warm, and giving. Whatever he did, wherever he went from here, he knew he would remember this day for the rest of his life.

Even before they left the idyllic spot, sparrows flitted from the trees to feast upon the crumbs. The greedy birds all but landed on Amanda's feet.

"Brave, aren't they?" she asked. "The crows will be along before we're back to the house. Then the sparrows are out of luck. It doesn't seem fair."

He wasn't surprised at yet more evidence of Amanda's soft heart. And though one part of him hated to disillusion her, the other part, the part grounded in reality, had him doing just that.

"Whatever made you think life was fair?"

Chapter Eight

Lucas didn't pretend to have the answers, but he'd promised Amanda his help.

He was good with figures. During his stint in vice, he'd learned to follow money trails. The bookkeeping of one boardinghouse should be a piece of cake.

Doggedly he sorted the papers, dividing them into neat piles of bills and receipts. Without Amanda there distracting him, the hours dragged by. Even though she provoked him, rattled him, and irritated him beyond reason because he couldn't ignore her, he missed her quick laugh and ready smile.

Two hours later, he pushed back the pile of bills, receipts, and bank statements that cluttered the kitchen table, which he had temporarily commandeered as his desk.

"She's trying to drive me crazy," he muttered. "Strike that. She's already done it." He resisted the urge to drop the whole mess into the trash can and simply write a check. The money meant nothing to him and would make the difference between Amanda keeping her home and losing it.

He wondered if someone had pulled an elaborate practical joke on him. Amanda's checkbook, while meticulously kept, showed a steady withdrawal of money with virtually none coming in. What happened to the rent from her boarders?

He was an ex-detective, not a magician. He couldn't make money appear where there was none. He made a note to ask Amanda about the missing rent checks.

An hour later, he threw the papers across the table, heedless of the mess he'd just made with what had taken him hours to organize.

He scanned the figures once more, certain he was mistaken. A second reading confirmed he hadn't been. He rattled off a string of curses that would have earned him an ear-boxing by his third-grade teacher.

For the last six months, Amanda had not received one cent from Rudy Goldblume in rent. From what he could piece together of her bank statements, the last payment from Rudy had been made sometime around the first of the year.

After making sure Amanda was occupied in the garden, he decided to confront Mr. Goldblume. He found him in the parlor playing solitaire. Lucas sat down beside him. "Mind if I join you?"

"Suit yourself."

He watched the gnarled hands slap down cards with surprising speed. "Mr. Goldblume—Rudy—I've been going over Amanda's books."

The elderly man looked up, his rheumy eyes warming appreciably at the mention of Amanda's name. "Amanda. She's the best thing that ever happened to me and Florence."

"Just how long do you intend to take advantage of Amanda's generosity?" The cop in him suspected the worst, but he couldn't reconcile that with the affection he saw in Rudy's eyes whenever he talked about Amanda.

A puzzled look now clouding his eyes, Rudy rubbed his jaw. "Take advantage?"

Lucas yanked back the sharp words that hovered on his tongue. "Receipts show you haven't paid rent in over six months."

"Amanda knows I'll pay her when my invention sells."

"What invention?"

"The one to recycle dryer lint. Of course, all my figures have to be theoretical so far, seeing as Amanda doesn't have a dryer."

Lucas stared. Rudy couldn't be serious. Recycled dryer lint? "When do you expect to finish this . . . invention?"

"In a month or so. Amanda knows. She said to take all the time I need."

Lucas believed it. She'd probably advanced him the money to get started.

Rudy smiled fondly. "Amanda believes in me. She's a good girl."

Lucas bit his tongue.

"Once my invention takes off, I'll repay Amanda everything I owe her. With interest."

This time Lucas couldn't keep silent. "Did you know Amanda's going to lose this house unless she can come up with some money? Fast."

He watched as Rudy's normally florid face paled.

"You didn't know, did you?"

"Amanda said not to worry about the money." Rudy pushed his glasses against his nose and stood, shoulders squared with the air of a man about to do things. "She always said we'd get by." He walked away, muttering, "I didn't know . . . I didn't know. . . ."

Lucas sank down on the old rocker, feeling like he'd just kicked a puppy. He'd guessed Rudy was just out for a free ride. Now that he knew differently, he didn't know what to do.

For years he'd relied on his instincts to keep him alive. Right now his instincts told him that though Rudy might be a little flaky, he was a decent man. *This house and its crazy inhabitants are getting to me,* Lucas thought in disgust. He shook his head at what he was about to do.

He knocked at Rudy's door and waited. He listened as the jazzy beat of "Boogie Woogie Bugle Boy of Company B" drifted through the door. Once more the feeling of falling through the looking glass returned.

Rudy opened the door, shoulders stooped, his customary smile conspicuously absent. His eyes were hollow, twin caves carved by guilt and anguish.

"Look, Rudy, I'm sorry for what I thought . . . I didn't realize . . . I'll loan you the money until your . . . invention sells."

The older man drew himself up. "I don't take charity. Never have, never will. Not even during the Depression. Caroline and I made do. Ate beans and corn bread for three years. You young folks don't know what hard times are." His eyes misted in remembrance before hardening as they once more rested on Lucas. "If you say Amanda's in trouble because of me, I'll find the money to pay her back, then clear out. Only honorable thing to do."

Lucas saw the open suitcase on the bed, a pitifully small stack of clothing next to it. He settled on the edge of the bed, pushing the clothes to one side. A carefully mended shirt snagged his attention. The shirt said more than words about Rudy's financial straits. And his pride.

The wave of tenderness that rolled through Lucas was as unfamiliar as what he was about to do. He had faced down hyped-up junkies and armed bank robbers, yet he hesitated when approaching this proud man whose very bearing dared Lucas to offer charity. He wondered what his buddies in the department would think if they could see him now.

He'd picked up a reputation on the job of being unflappable and totally without mercy when it came to the bad guys. His second partner had dubbed him "Reed 'Em and Weep." The nickname had stuck and had followed him from vice to homicide.

A man—a cop—had only so much emotional energy. If he expended it on every tragedy, every cruelty he witnessed, he'd burn out within a month. Still, he couldn't let Rudy leave. Not only would Amanda never forgive him, he strongly suspected he'd never be able to forgive himself.

"It's not charity," Lucas said again and resisted the urge to wipe his brow. He couldn't let Rudy see how important this was to him. "You got anything against making a business deal?"

Rudy gave Lucas a suspicious look. "Depends."

"That's all a loan is. A business deal. I'll even draw up a contract, if you like. Charge you interest."

A slow smile spread across the wrinkled face, only to fade and be replaced by a frown. "Can't let you do it."

"Think of all the interest I'll collect," Lucas said, keeping his voice properly grave.

Rudy rubbed his chin. "Well, if you put it that way, maybe we could work something out." He held out his hand with quiet dignity.

With equal dignity, Lucas shook the wrinkled hand.

"This is right nice of you, son. Right nice." Then Rudy gave an embarrassed snort. "You'll have to excuse me. Bladder's not what it used to be."

"Sure," Lucas said. Rudy was already shuffling toward the bathroom.

After a hurried call to his accountant, Lucas drew up a simple contract. "This is just between us," he said when Rudy returned. "We don't want Amanda to know."

"Why not?"

Lucas searched for a plausible answer, wondering whether he was trying to convince Rudy or himself. "Because she might worry. We don't want that."

Rudy tapped his finger to the side of his nose. "You're

right. Amanda would worry. She's a nice girl. Always thinking of others." He regarded Lucas with sharp eyes. "You're a right nice feller. Too bad you live in the city. Never could abide cities. No heart to 'em. They ain't got no heart a'tall."

No heart.

The words echoed through Lucas' mind for the remainder of the day. Was that what was wrong with his life? No heart? He thought of his condominium, decorated by one of the city's top design firms. Predominately chrome and glass with stark white carpet and walls.

Unbidden, the image of his room at Amanda's house, with its four-poster bed and ceramic giraffe, appeared in his mind. No one could accuse it of lacking personality. It was the same in all the rooms of the house. They reflected Amanda—her warmth, her humor, her essence.

"You're losing it, man," he said, his voice harsh against the silence. "You're losing it big-time."

It couldn't be put off any longer.

Discovering how Amanda supported Rudy was easy. It had taken a little more digging to unearth how she was subsidizing her other boarder. He still couldn't believe it as he stared at receipts for dentures and cataract surgery. Instead of bringing in money by renting out rooms, Amanda was actually losing money. Then again, knowing her as he did, he ought to have guessed why so much money was going out and so little coming in. Now he had to confront her with what he'd found out.

He caught her just as she was on her way to the barn. "We need to talk."

"Can't it wait?"

"No." Frustration added an edge to his voice.

Her eyebrows rose, but she settled on the porch swing.

He held up a receipt. "What's this for?"

She glanced at it. "Dentures."

Her casual tone didn't fool him. "I can see it's for dentures. You don't wear dentures." He paused. "Do you?"

"Of course I don't wear dentures. They're for Florence."

"But why did you pay for them?"

All at once, she appeared uncomfortable. "She gave me some cash, and I wrote a check for them."

"Amanda, you're the poorest liar I've ever known."

Her chin jutted out. "All right. I paid for them. When she lost her other set of dentures, she wouldn't even come out of her room, she was so embarrassed. She couldn't eat anything but baby food. I couldn't let her starve, could I?"

She didn't say any more, but he could hear her thoughts as clearly as if she'd spoken them aloud. *So there. What are you going to do about it?*

He wanted to take her in his arms and kiss her; he also wanted to shake some sense into her. It was yet another reminder that Amanda came with all kinds of strings.

It all sounded perfectly reasonable. She'd dug herself neatly into debt. How was he supposed to dig her out again? "What about her family? Florence showed me pictures of her daughter and grandchildren."

Amanda smiled sadly. "Did you look closely at those pictures?"

"No . . ."

"They're more than fifteen years old. Her family hasn't been in touch with her for at least that long."

"How do you know?"

"I talked with the social worker who worked at the retirement home where she lived before she came here. In all the time she lived there, she never had a visitor, not even a letter. The only mail she ever gets here is her Social Security check. It barely covers her prescriptions."

Lucas wanted to swear. He wanted to hit something. Preferably *someone*. He settled for slamming his fist into his open palm.

"How can children stop loving their parents?" A fierce light glowed on her face, and the heat of it toughened her voice. He knew she'd fight to protect her elderly boarders. He'd spent the first half of his life wishing for parents to love him and the second convincing himself that he was better off without anyone. Danny's death had only confirmed that.

He gathered her to him, wishing he could protect her from what he'd learned early in life: love was an illusion. He held her, not knowing what else to do. His experience in offering comfort was limited at best. "They get too busy with their own lives, their own problems," he said at last.

"Have you noticed how Rudy checks the mail every day?"

Lucas nodded. He'd seen Rudy shuffling out to the porch, waiting impatiently for the mail to arrive. Holidays brought on a deep depression for Rudy because they meant no mail delivery.

"Do you know what he does afterward? He goes back to his bedroom and rocks in his chair. I knocked on his door one time and found him that way. I tried talking with him, but he wouldn't answer. He just kept rocking. Then, a couple of hours later, he was back down in the basement, working on his invention, like nothing had happened."

Lucas blinked rapidly. Must be something in the air. His eyes felt watery, sensitive. The tears that fell were foreign to him. He wiped his cheek and looked in wonder at the drops that clung to his fingers.

She brought his finger to her lips and sucked away the tear. "It's all right to have feelings, Lucas," she said, her voice soothing his raw emotions with the balm of her understanding.

"Says who?" But the joke fell flat, and he winced. He sounded like he was begging for sympathy.

"Me."

He captured her hand in his own, bringing it to his mouth. "What are we going to do about Rudy and Florence?"

"Do?"

"You can't keep supporting them."

"I thought you understood—"

Lucas held up a hand. "I'm not suggesting you throw them out. I'm trying to come up with a way you can keep your house."

"Rudy's invention—"

"To recycle dryer lint?" This time Lucas' smile was genuine. "You don't really believe in that, do you?"

Amanda smiled too. "Maybe. It could work, couldn't it?"

"Not in a million years. I'm afraid we're going to have to do better than that."

They spent the next hour trying out ideas, some of them serious, others hilarious. Lucas forgot his self-appointed task to straighten out her finances as he tried to outdo Amanda in outrageousness.

"You're crazy," he said at her last suggestion that they invent a toilet seat that beeped if it wasn't lowered.

"It's the company I keep." She leaned over to brush her lips against his.

He kissed her. Softly. Sweetly. Tenderly. And Lucas knew he had been caught in a trap of his own making.

When Rudy handed Amanda a check for back rent, she simply stared. He folded her fingers over it.

"I'm sorry I'm so late getting this to you, Amanda. I didn't know—" Abruptly, he cut short whatever he'd been about to say.

She scarcely gave the check a glance, expecting a token payment on his rent. When the amount registered, she barely contained her surprise. In her hand was six months' rent.

"But how did you—"

"It's all there," he said. "You can count it. If I'd known . . ."

"I don't need to count it. If you'd known what?" she prompted gently.

"Nothing." He shuffled from foot to foot.

"You're sure you can afford this right now? If not, I can—"

"I can afford it just fine. You've been carrying me too long as it is." He kept his gaze fixed on the floor, clearly reluctant to meet her eyes.

Her curiosity aroused, she was about to press the issue, when she realized she'd only add to his discomfort.

"You're a real sweet girl, worrying yourself about an old man like me. You ought to be spending your time sparking. Maybe with that young feller in there." He jerked his finger toward the kitchen, where Lucas was working. "He ain't bad, for a city feller."

"You're not old," she declared, ignoring the heavy-handed hint about Lucas.

"Thank you for that." He kissed her cheek, and she caught a whiff of Old Spice and peppermint. As he walked away, she noticed he held his shoulders a little straighter than before.

Where had he gotten the money? As far as she knew, he had no income other than his Social Security checks. And why his persistence in paying her today? She hadn't shared her money worries with anyone but Florence. And Lucas.

The pieces fell into place. Lucas must have told Rudy

about her plight. A slow anger kindled inside her as she thought of him bothering Rudy for back rent. If he'd badgered her boarder about money . . . She shook her head as the theory fell short. It still didn't explain the money. Unless . . .

Her anger ebbed as she realized what must have happened.

Her heart did a slow tumble in her chest before settling into a quiet joy. *Lucas Reed, you're a fraud,* she thought. *A gold-plated fraud. And you've just been found out.* The self-proclaimed cynic had a heart as soft as her own. He was a puzzle she doubted she'd ever unravel.

She hugged her newfound knowledge to her, and a smile curled around her heart. She'd keep his secret. For now anyway.

Outside, the moon continued its nightly ride across the sky. Somewhere in a tree an owl hooted. A woodland animal called to its mate. And inside, Amanda fell effortlessly, sumptuously in love with Lucas all over again.

Amanda had been acting strange late.

Not that she hadn't been acting strange already; after all, her whole household was strange. This was a different kind of strange. *Good analysis, Reed. The lady's got you so tied in knots that you can't even think about her without getting muddled.*

If he didn't know better, he'd say she knew of his little loan to Rudy. He'd sworn Rudy to secrecy and didn't believe he would break his promise to keep the transaction just between the two of them.

Still, Amanda had been smiling more than usual, the kind of smile that said *I know something you don't know.*

He wasn't given time to ponder on that as, amid a flurry of scarves and beads, Florence flowed into the kitchen and zeroed in on Lucas. "Thank you."

He looked perplexed.

"Rudy told me what you did for him." She turned to Amanda. "You wouldn't know, but Lucas here lent Rudy money to pay his rent for the last few months."

Her breezy smile took in both of them. "Rudy told me. I know all about the promise he made to Lucas. I had to pry it out of him." She chuckled.

Lucas didn't even crack a smile. Only the tiny nerve that pulsed in his jaw betrayed any emotion.

"You've a good heart." Florence reached up to plant a kiss on his cheek.

He didn't move. It was as though he didn't know how to respond.

Amanda's heart ached for the man who didn't know how to accept gratitude.

For the first time in the weeks since he'd come to Sweetbriar, he made an awkward move. He wrapped his arm around Florence and held her close. The gesture was jerky, clumsy, and all the more endearing because of it.

Florence smiled widely and returned the hug.

Amanda wiped moisture from her eyes. She felt a jolt of pleasure that Lucas wasn't unmoved. They were getting to him, she thought. She and the others. He had so much to offer. If he could only see himself as she did.

Once Florence left, Amanda hugged him. "Thank you."

He shrugged. "It was no big deal."

The ex-cop was attractive enough to turn any woman's head, but it was his simple kindness that had won her heart. She smiled at this loving man, so unsure of himself and trying his best to navigate the uncharted world of caring about others.

Her lips straightened into a determined line. "You're a good man. It's time you realized it."

"You don't know what you're saying." A flicker of irritation ran across his face. When she looked deeper, she saw that it wasn't irritation but embarrassment.

"I was brought up on stories of knights-errant and fair damsels. I was dreaming of heroes performing courageous deeds while all the other little girls were playing Charlie's Angels."

"I'm no hero." A line worked its way between his eyebrows, a sure sign that he was going all male and stubborn on her.

"How do you know?"

"Because . . . heroes are . . . heroic."

She smiled inside. "I'm an authority on heroes, and I say you are one." She reached up to trace his lips, her fingers lingering there. She felt the tension in him, part of him straining to pull away while the other yearned to give in to her. Holding her breath, she waited.

"I'm not a knight in shining armor," he said, scowling. "I'm just a man. And not a very nice one at that."

"I don't believe you."

"Believe it. I'm not what you need."

"How do you know what I need?" she asked with a lightness she was far from feeling.

"You need someone who'll be around for the long haul. You need someone who wants the same things you do—a home and family. That's not me. Don't make me into something I'm not. It's not fair. To either of us."

He was no longer scowling. Now he looked scared. Worse than scared. He looked trapped.

She couldn't argue with him, not when he so obviously believed what he said. Regret washed over her. Though she didn't want to debate the issue, she was prepared to go into battle if need be. Because the way he looked at her when he didn't think she was watching . . . It didn't happen often. Mostly when he was exhausted or his leg was bothering him.

She knew he'd shy away from any talk of feelings, especially love. So she'd keep her feelings to herself. For now. But Lucas loved her. She knew it as surely as she did that she loved him.

"I wish I'd known you sooner, Amanda Clayson. Things might have been different."

The wistful note in his voice wasn't lost on her.

A sigh rippled through her. She'd lost the battle. But that didn't mean she was going to lose the war.

Chapter Nine

This wasn't the day she'd find the key to healing the scars of Lucas' past, Amanda thought with regret. All she could do was love him and pray that her knight in shining armor would someday realize that a bit of tarnish didn't detract from that love.

She'd been right. He did look trapped. Trapped between what he wanted and what, for reasons she understood but didn't accept, he wouldn't allow himself to have.

For the rest of the afternoon, she kept things light. She'd find a way to convince him that he not only needed love but that he deserved it.

When the rest of the household retired, she and Lucas ate chocolate chip cookies on the porch. He started in on his third, the gleeful expression on his face that of an overgrown boy. "Ambrosia." He patted his flat stomach. "If I hang around here much longer, I'm going to need a personal trainer. These cookies are incredible." He looked at her wonderingly. "Cookies . . . cookies," he repeated, his voice rising.

"Glad you like them. I experimented and added white-chocolate chips."

He made an impatient sound. "What do you love most in the world?"

Besides you? The words were nearly out before she choked them back. "My family."

"Aside from them."

She didn't have to think about it. "Chocolate."

"Put it to work for you. Make and sell your own gourmet candies, cookies, cakes. I could name a dozen people right now who'd pay through the nose for cookies like these." As if to prove his point, he reached for another one.

"People don't buy chocolate chip cookies. They make them. At home."

He kissed her. "Sweetheart, you've got a lot to learn." He'd moved among the rich and famous enough to know they'd ante up for anything if it came in the right packaging with an outrageous price. Add that to a truly superior product, and you had a winner.

They brainstormed over a name. It was Lucas who came up with the winner. *Sweet Bites.*

For a week, he ignored his writing and worked with Amanda to come up a business plan. The next step was to convince a banker to catch the same vision.

With that goal, they made a trip to the local bank.

"Mr. Reed, Ms. Clayson." Nils Larsson, the vice president, rose, gestured for them to be seated, and resettled his considerable bulk in his chair behind the desk. "What can we do for you today?"

Nerves danced in her belly as Amanda laid out plans for the business of selling gourmet chocolates.

"You want to sell chocolate?" The trace of amusement in the man's voice was enough to set her teeth on edge, but she kept her smile in place.

"Gourmet chocolates," she said. "I plan to cater to the upscale market." She and Lucas had agreed she would be the one to present the specifics of the plan. She pointed to the detailed strategy, complete with projected figures that Lucas had prepared. "As you can see, the market for gourmet chocolates and related items is increasing. I have the skills. All I need is start-up money."

Mr. Larsson scratched his head. "You've presented a strong case, but a project like this requires more than a little baking. It needs business know-how." He stood, circled the desk, and perched on its edge. "I like you, Amanda. I liked your great-aunt. Much as I admire you, you've got no experience in running a business."

She had no answer to that. He was right.

"She's got me," Lucas said.

Did she? She didn't have a chance to ponder on that as the banker gave Lucas a speculative look.

"Are you planning on co-signing for Ms. Clayson?"

Amanda straightened in her chair. She had to be the one to make this work. She chose her words carefully. "Of course I'm grateful for Lucas'—Mr. Reed's help, but I'm responsible for my debts."

Out of the corner of her eye, she caught Lucas' smile of approval.

Mr. Larsson steepled his fingers across his paunch. "As I said, Amanda, you're not—"

"You've known me ever since I was a kid and visited Aunt Roxy in the summers. And you know me well enough to know I keep my word. I intend on making this work. With or without your help. If your bank can't help me, I'll go somewhere else."

She felt Lucas' fingers close around her own. Gratefully, she returned the gentle pressure.

The banker scanned the reports once more. He seemed to come to some kind of decision. "You may have a workable plan here. I'll approach the board of directors, get their take on it."

The tepid words were not the stuff of dreams, but Amanda grabbed on to them. She stood and clasped his outstretched hand. "Thank you."

"You were great back there," Lucas said once they were in the car.

"Thanks." She drew a shaky breath. "What if they still turn us down?"

"Then we go to another bank. Just like you told him."

His confidence was contagious. "I'm going to make this work."

Riding high on their success, they celebrated. A drive through the mountains. Dinner in a fancy restaurant—a dinner she didn't have to cook. Extravagant plans for how she would spend the money they were certain she would make.

She felt jumpy with energy, the quicksilver kind that

had her taking Lucas' hands and whirling around in the restaurant's parking lot. Oblivious to onlookers, they danced until she fell against him, holding her sides.

"Come on," he said. "I'm taking you home."

When they reached Sweetbriar, she reached up to cup his face between her palms. "Thank you. For everything."

"Don't thank me yet. Owning your own business is no picnic. By the time you get this off the ground, you may be ready to strangle me."

Amanda had cause to remember his words two days later when Mr. Larsson called and gave her the news that the loan was approved.

"I'm going to need both of you," she said to Rudy and Florence. Their smiles of delight warmed her through and through.

Starting up a business required more work than she'd ever imagined. By the end of the first week, she fell into bed every night exhausted but happy. The best part was that the whole household was involved. She couldn't have done it without Lucas. He was quietly there, advising, suggesting, but never attempting to take over. For that, as well as a thousand other things, she was grateful.

Only one thing cast a shadow over her happiness. She woke up every morning terrified that this would be the day Lucas told her good-bye. She hoarded their days together, holding them close to her heart. They were more precious than gold.

They made a trip to the county seat to register her

business name with the county clerk, placed advertisements in the various papers, and had cards and letterhead printed.

Her resolve wavered a bit when the bills started arriving. "All this money . . . and I haven't sold a thing yet."

"You have to spend money to make money," Lucas reminded her. "You're a businesswoman now. It's time to start acting like one."

Her confidence grew as orders began pouring in during the following weeks, many of them bearing instructions to ship to California addresses. "How did—" *Lucas. Of course.* "You asked your friends to buy from me, didn't you?" she asked.

He gave an innocent smile. "I shipped samples to some friends in Hollywood. The cookies themselves did the selling. That and a little word of mouth."

"At this rate, we'll have to hire more help," Amanda said.

"You've got us," Florence said.

Amanda looked up from where she was twirling ribbon into a bow before securing it around a container of chocolate chip–macadamia nut cookies. "I couldn't do it without you and Rudy."

With the business taking off like wildfire, she could barely keep up with the demand for her products. Another six months and she should be out of debt with maybe a little left over. She spent a few moments entertaining delicious ways of spending the profits. The idea of having money not already spoken for was a luxury she'd never allowed herself to dream of.

And she owed it all to Lucas. Without his expertise and guidance, she'd never have made it. Her thoughts took her full circle. Back to Lucas.

By evening, they had filled the outstanding orders. Flushed with success, she started on a special dessert for the family. When Lucas showed up after a trip to town, she held out a spoon for him to taste.

"Mmm." He licked the spoon, then kissed her. He tasted of chocolate and man. "You've been busy." He trailed a finger down her cheek.

"I get a lot done without distractions." She took his hand and brought it to her lips.

"When you finish here, can I distract you?"

"I'm counting on it."

Her sigh was interrupted as gentle hands swept her hair from her neck. A featherlight kiss landed on her nape.

"Mmm." She turned to meet Lucas' lips with her own.

He lowered his head and grazed her lips with his own, sending sparks snapping down her nerve ends.

Kisses as soft as angel wings skimmed over her. His taste filled her senses like the darkest of chocolates. She forgot to breathe. Air escaped in a whoosh when he raised his head. One kiss was too many, she thought with a wild desire to laugh, and a million would never be enough. In that scrap of time, a fragment of a moment, something eternal happened, and she knew she wasn't the same woman of a few minutes ago.

Her happiness deflated a bit when she caught him

looking at her oddly, as if he had something to tell her and didn't know how to proceed. A moment later, she decided she must have imagined it, for he gave her one of those smiles that warmed her inside and out.

They celebrated that night. Champagne and chocolate. Lucas provided the Champagne, Amanda the chocolate. Like two guilty schoolchildren, they slipped out of the house and met on the porch.

"To us," she toasted.

Gently, Lucas tapped his glass to hers. "To you. Amanda Clayson, entrepreneur."

The demands of the day finally caught up with her, and she drifted into a light sleep.

Lucas watched as Amanda slept on the porch swing, tucked at his side. He pushed the hair from her face and studied her. She was beautiful, inside and out.

Moonlight spilled over her face, highlighting the curve of her mouth, turned up in a smile even in sleep. He felt his heart move in his chest. Shouldn't he be accustomed to her effect on him by now?

He shifted on the swing, a half smile touching his lips as he gazed at the patchwork quilt that covered them. Like the rest of the house, the quilt had a homey feel that was a world away from his condo, where every item had been chosen with the utmost care from upscale stores.

Amanda fit here, with the old quilts, sprigs of lilac tucked in unexpected places, and a dog who actually slept on his bed if given the slightest encouragement. While he, with his obscenely expensive sports car and the latest in laptops, was an interloper.

Despite those feelings—or maybe because of them—his writing was back on track. The words spilled from his mind and onto the page with almost ridiculous ease. The book, which he'd once despaired over, was nearing completion.

He'd e-mailed several chapters to his agent. "I don't know what you're doing," Jerry had said, "but keep it up. This stuff is gold."

Amanda and her household had turned him around. She was the only woman he'd ever known who could wear down his edge, completely disarm him. He was accustomed to being in control of his emotions, but Amanda Clayson simply climbed over the hurdles he'd erected and plowed straight through to the heart he'd believed had frozen solid.

He'd intended to stay detached. Had tried to. Tried and failed. Bit by bit, he'd allowed himself to fall under the spell she wove.

For a while, he'd let himself believe that he had finally found his way out of the mire of guilt and pain of his past. With Amanda and the others, he'd actually believed that he had started to heal.

He realized he'd only been fooling himself. The wounds were still oozing. He ripped off the scabs every time he allowed memories of Danny to slip back into his mind, every time he put words onto a page.

She wanted more than he'd ever given anyone. She wanted commitment, and there was nothing that terrified him more.

Once more, he thought of the contrast between his outlook on life and Amanda's. He was darkness, his whole being shaded with it. Amanda was light and life. Wonderful, abundant life. It filled her so beautifully, so totally, that it was seeping from her.

It was time, he knew, past time to do some clear thinking. He'd known Amanda for less than two months, but he'd allowed himself to care for her more than any other woman who had touched his life.

He had let things go too far. He refused to let Amanda down as he had Danny. He needed to leave Sweetbriar, to leave Amanda before things went any further. The words to tell her formed in his brain but refused to form on his tongue.

She stirred, then looked up at him with eyes filled with love.

He pressed his lips to her temple. And what moved inside him had no place there.

Chapter Ten

Amanda made her plans.

She knew it was calculated. But, after all, what was wrong with that? Preparation and presentation, they were part of any recipe. Every cook knew the importance of timing. Leave a cake in the oven too long and you had a brick. Too little time and you had mush.

So if she chose her moment on a night when the sky glimmered with stars and the air was redolent with the smell of freshly mowed grass, it was only common sense.

The day had been touched with magic. They'd played hooky, taking a picnic into the mountains and spending hours doing nothing but being together. It had been Lucas' idea, and that gave her courage.

She set the stage as carefully as any master chef preparing for a particularly delectable dessert. Ingredients and tools, whether in the kitchen or out, it was essential to choose the best.

Candles, dozens of them. Fresh flowers.

The scene was perfect. The man who sat across the

table from her was imperfect, and she loved him all the more for it.

He was a hero. For only a hero could make the leap from a pain-filled past to a loving future. *A future.* Funny how two small words could hold so much meaning.

They could make a life together. A wonderful, crazy, beautiful life filled with love and laughter and the un-avoidable pain that came with being human. She could hardly wait.

She looked up at him, letting all she felt for him shine through in her eyes. She wanted him to see it. To see everything. To know everything. To understand that she loved him and that he loved her.

Love, hot and sweet, welled up inside her. She took a chance and said what was in her heart. "I love you."

He took her hand and cradled it within his own. "Amanda . . ."

She heard the hitch in his breath, the husky note in his voice that told her everything she needed to know. She looked at their joined hands. They fit so well, she thought, just slid together, as if they'd been made for that sole purpose.

She felt, more than heard, his sharp intake of breath. She waited, hoping, praying.

Because the words would not be denied now that they were out in the open, she said them again. "I love you."

Time ground to a standstill. Along with her heart-beat.

"I can't give you what you want," he said.

"Even if all I want is to tell you that I love you?"

Silence surrounded them, its heavy thickness a weight that neither could shrug off.

Lucas was the first to break it. "I'm leaving tomorrow."

He said it so quietly that the words didn't register at first.

"But today . . ."

"I wanted to have one last day with you, make one more memory." He shoved a hand through his hair. "I've finished the book and sent it off to my agent. That was my reason for coming here," he reminded her.

"So today was your way of telling me good-bye." The irony of it struck her. She'd been basking in a brightness of hope, and all along he'd been preparing to leave her. "Because of what I said?" The words scratched her throat raw.

"Because of what I can't say. I'm no Prince Charming."

"It doesn't matter. What matters is that I love you and you love me."

"Amanda—"

"I know you love me." She couldn't have been mistaken in that.

"You don't get it, do you? I do not love you." He spaced each word with a deliberateness that made her cringe. "I'm too selfish, too set in my ways to love anyone."

"You'd rather believe you're running away because you're selfish than because you're scared. You're better than that, Lucas. At least I thought you were." She couldn't imagine running away from home and sanctuary. And love. Then she realized that she had done exactly that when she'd left her family. But she'd made a new home here at Sweetbriar. She'd thought Lucas had as well.

She changed tactics. A good cook knew the value of flexibility. "Did you ever wonder about why you came here?"

He lifted a shoulder. "I came across your Web site. It sounded like what I needed."

"Maybe you were meant to come here."

"I'll bite. For what?"

She hesitated. He wasn't going to like this. "Because you were wounded and needed healing."

He tapped his right leg. "My leg healed years ago. It's as good as it's going to get."

"I'm not talking about your leg." She paused. "Your spirit needed healing. Your life."

"My life's just fine."

"Your life is so sterile that you're afraid to let a feeling inside. You're so afraid to admit you might have feelings that you'd do anything to hide them."

"You're way off the mark!"

His anger fueled her determination to convince him otherwise. "Am I? Everything that happens, happens for a purpose. Why is it so hard to believe that you were brought here for a reason?"

"You know why I came here."

"I know why you think you came." Hope was slowly slipping away, but she had to try.

"You're talking in riddles."

"Maybe."

"Be careful. You're starting to sound like Florence."

"Despite everything, Florence still believes in life. In love."

"Don't start practicing your miracles on me, Amanda. I'm immune."

"Just like you're immune to love. Right?"

"I'm not immune to it. I just don't believe it exists."

"It does for us," she said.

"There isn't any *us*," he said quietly, hating himself for saying the words, hating her for making him say them.

She only stared at him, as though his words hadn't registered.

With more strength than he believed he possessed, he pulled away from her, trying to ignore the hurt that flared in her eyes.

"Don't." The single word flayed his already raw emotions. "Don't push me away." The plea in her voice almost caused him to relent. Almost.

"I can't."

"Can't what? Can't want me? Can't need me? Can't love me?" Curbed frustration marked her voice.

He gave a jerky nod.

She no longer tried to hide the hurt in her eyes. It broke his heart. "Why not?"

"You know why," he said in a low voice.

"Because you're afraid. Not good enough." The beginnings of anger trickled through the words.

"You don't have any right—"

"I have all the right in the world. I love you." The stark words, thrown as a gauntlet, challenged him, taunted him, warmed him. It was the last that was the hardest to resist.

It couldn't matter. He couldn't let it matter.

He had no choice. He had to make his stand now. Or lose the very essence of himself. He was drowning in his feelings for her. Some of what he felt for her must have shown in his eyes, for he saw the flicker of hope in hers.

For the fleetest of moments, his resolve faltered. Amanda made him want to believe. In her. In them. In love.

The hope glowed deeper in her eyes. Ironically, that served to harden his heart. What would it do to her, to him, if and when he proved that he was right about himself? He couldn't risk it.

The light went out of her eyes. And his heart.

"Because of Danny?"

He didn't answer. He didn't have to.

"We've been through this. You weren't to blame for Danny's death."

What was she trying to do? Offer him absolution? If that was what Amanda had in mind, she was wrong. If he'd been quicker, maybe his partner would be alive today. *If* . . . How he hated that word.

"Do you think you've got the market cornered on guilt? I've got news for you. There's plenty of it to go around."

"It's not that simple."

"Life's never simple. But love is."

He stared at Amanda. How could he leave this woman? How could he not?

"I love you," she repeated.

They were the most humbling words a man could hear. If only he were the right man. For a moment, he was tempted, sorely tempted, to promise her anything as long as she would continue looking at him as she did just now. Maybe then he could become the man she thought he was. As swiftly as the thought formed, he rejected it. Amanda deserved more than his feeble attempts at trying to return her love.

Her laugh came out in a strangled sob. "You know what's funny? You already love me. I see it in your eyes. I feel it when you touch me. But you can't say the words. You can't force yourself to say them because if you did, you'd be vulnerable like the rest of us. And that's the one thing you can't be, the one thing you won't let yourself be.

"I love you, Lucas. I always will. Nothing's going to change that. Not even you." She wasn't finished with him. "I'm not going to apologize for loving you. I'm not asking for anything but that you believe me when I say I love you." When he remained silent, she shook her head. "But even that's too much, isn't it?"

Why couldn't it be simple, Lucas wondered. Fictional stories thrived upon complications and conflict, but he preferred things simple in real life.

He should have seen it coming. For a woman like Amanda, romance and love were synonymous. She couldn't have one without feeling the other. She was an idealist, believing in the basic goodness of people. In his case, that belief was definitely misplaced.

Greedily he'd accepted what she gave so freely, basking in her sweetness, soaking up the warmth that spread to anyone who entered the magic circle she spun around her. Now it was time to pay up. That it was ripping the soul from him was only right. He deserved that . . . and more. She'd laid her heart bare, offering him the most precious gift a man could desire. And what did he do? Threw it back in her face.

She reached for him. He caught her hand before she could touch him. He didn't trust himself. "Find yourself someone who can give you what you need."

"I already have."

It was too much for him, because he knew he didn't deserve her. "You'd be throwing your life away on me."

She laughed, a pain-filled huff of air. "Why? Because you're not perfect? No one expects you to be. And even if you were, there are things you can't control. So you fail, and when you do, it drives you crazy, and you beat yourself up and blame yourself. Even though it's not your fault."

"Don't you get it? I'm not the man you think I am. That man died in a stinking alley along with his partner." And he didn't know if he'd ever be able to find him again.

"What I understand is that you want things to be easy. Well, life isn't easy. It's hard. But you wouldn't know about that." Hectic red flags unfurled on her cheeks as she defied his self-description.

His laugh was a harsh rasp. "I figured that out for myself when Danny died."

"Did you? You're still looking for the easy way out. And you chose guilt. You wear it like a hair shirt. It's your way of keeping the rest of the world out. It's too easy. But that's what you want, isn't it? To bury yourself in guilt. To wallow in it so that you don't have to face the risks of living. And loving." Tears were raw in her stomach, but she refused to give way to them.

"You don't know—"

"It's you who doesn't know! You don't have the courage to face what's out there." She spread her arms wide. "You gave up on life. You gave up on yourself. It's too bad, because there's a great big world out there that needs you. You! Just as you are. Imperfect and flawed."

Lucas hurt all over. A bone-deep hurt that had nothing to do with his injured leg and everything to do with what he saw in Amanda's eyes.

He found refuge in brusqueness. "Everything's set up at the bank. Mr. Larsson has agreed to give you the extension as long as you keep up the payments. Once the business takes off, you shouldn't have any problems. If you do, give me a call."

"Thank you," Amanda said with the politeness of a stranger, "but I don't think that'll be necessary."

He ignored the small stab of hurt and pressed on. "The new brochures ought to be arriving in the next week or two. Once they do, mail them out. I left a mailing list on the computer. All you need—"

"We've gone over this already," she pointed out gently.

He was stalling. He knew it. Anything to postpone saying what needed to be said. His brain scrambled for something else, something he'd forgotten to tell her, anything to avoid the inevitable.

He let his gaze find hers. Her eyes held no accusation, only a heart-splintering sadness. Her delicate mouth was shadowed with the same pain, pain he had put there.

His humorless smile was a razor acceptance of the futility of dreams.

"I love you," she said.

He said nothing, only waited for words of reproach, words he deserved to hear, but there were none. For one long, aching minute, he simply looked at her and wished he could put everything right. "If things were different . . ." He let the words trail off because they both knew it wasn't *things* that needed to be different.

It was him.

He started to reach for her, needing that last contact, but she jerked away, as though his very touch would scald her. With an effort, he kept his hands at his sides. His gaze found hers. Her eyes held no surprise, only grief.

"We've spent a lot of time talking about what you want. What about what I want? What I need? Did you stop to think of that, even once?"

Shame coursed through him.

"Go," she said, her voice so soft, it reached him only because he strained to hear it. "Run away."

"That's not fair."

"Maybe not. But it's true. You're running away from love. A word you can't even say."

He wanted to argue with her. He wasn't running away. He'd never run from anything in his life. But arguments had no place in good-byes. "Amanda."

"You're right. You don't deserve me." Her voice held a quiet dignity, at odds with the pain shimmering in her eyes, luminous with unshed tears. "I need a partner, a husband. Not a shell of a man who's too afraid to live. And love." Her lips trembled once, twice, then firmed.

Amanda needed a strong man, one who could stand beside her, not cower in fear because he couldn't let go of the past.

But that man wasn't him.

His hands balled into fists at his sides. The anger building inside him wasn't directed at her but at himself. He knew if he reached for her again, his hands would tremble, so great was his need to touch her. He wanted her with a longing so acute that it was a physical ache. And he knew he couldn't have her.

A tear squeezed out of the corner of her eye and slid down her cheek. He caught it on the tip of his finger and watched as it dissolved at his touch, as ephemeral as a snowflake. Like his chance for happiness? He dismissed the idea as fanciful.

"Forgive me," he whispered.

"No." The uncompromising word shredded emotions already ragged with pain, and he flinched.

She was silent for long moments. There was nothing

gentle in her tone when she finally spoke. "No. I won't forgive you for denying both of us a chance at happiness. People look all their lives for what we have together. And you're willing to throw it away."

The disgust in her voice caused him to shrivel inwardly.

She was right. Of course she was right. And he was powerless to do anything about it.

He tried again, though he didn't know what he hoped to do.

"Amanda . . ."

She faced him, her eyes so achingly beautiful that he had no idea how he managed to stand there without screaming with the pain of what he had to do.

"You're so busy pretending to be noble that you don't even know what you're missing. Someday you'll believe me," she said. "Someday you'll accept how I feel, and you won't doubt any longer. You'll think of me. You'll remember. And you'll wonder what we could have had together . . . if you weren't afraid."

He ached with the pain he saw in Amanda's eyes.

The tears were coming faster now. They trickled unchecked down her cheeks, glistening against her skin.

Her tears, as always, stopped him. He had no weapons against them. He paused. "I wish—"

"You don't have to wish."

The steadiness of her voice shamed him. Even now, with tears streaming down her cheeks, she was the strong one.

"Good-bye, Amanda," he said, knowing he was saying good-bye to more than her. He was saying good-bye to the only true happiness he'd ever known.

He imprinted on his memory the curve of her jaw, the sheen of her hair, the shape of her mouth. And then he walked away.

Florence cornered him in the kitchen. "I found Amanda crying in her room. She told me you were leaving."

He sighed and prepared to take his medicine.

"You're either a coward or a fool."

Lucas clamped down on his anger, biting back the desire to tell her to mind her own business. For one thing, he couldn't bring himself to be rude to her. For another, he didn't think it would do any good. Florence Wanlass lived on her own terms and by her own rules.

"A sweet little girl like Amanda loves you. You ought to be down on your knees thanking sweet heaven for her. Instead, you're going to throw it all away." Her mouth pinched at the corners, and color slashed high on her cheeks.

Lucas felt the weight of her disapproval pressing down on his shoulders, forcing another sigh from him. He was too weary to defend his position, too discouraged to care that Florence might be right.

"What do I do?" He hadn't realized he'd voiced the question aloud.

"You don't need me telling you what your heart already knows." A hint of sympathy softened the sharpness of the words.

He ignored it. "My heart's got nothing to do with it."

"Oh, I think it has everything to do with it," she said, and her mouth crumpled. "The heart's a wondrous thing. Strong enough to withstand an attack but fragile enough to be broken by an unkind word." She pressed her mouth to his cheek. When she pulled back, there were tears in her eyes. "We'll miss you, boy. We'll all miss you."

They weren't finished with him. Rudy showed up next. "You did me a favor, and I owe you. That doesn't mean I aim to sit by while you break Amanda's heart."

Lucas resigned himself to another lecture.

Rudy had something else in mind. He planted one on Lucas' jaw. Pain sang through him.

The man was more than twice his age and half his weight. No way could Lucas defend himself. So he stood there while Rudy landed a fist on the other side of his jaw.

Rudy stomped off, leaving Lucas to stare after him and rub his face. A soft, clear whistle drew his attention outside. Unable to help himself, he followed the sound. He searched the porch and yard but found nothing. Fairies, Amanda would tell him.

Heaven help him, he was afraid if he stayed here any longer, he'd start believing in them himself. And if he believed in fairies, he might even come to believe in love.

Amanda deserved a man brave enough to risk his heart, but there were risks he feared he'd never have the courage to take again. And with Amanda, he was afraid—terribly afraid—that the cost of that risk was the price of his soul. He couldn't give her what he knew she wanted. He couldn't give what he didn't have.

Amanda swiped at the tears that dampened her cheeks. Why was she crying? Because Lucas had left? That was a no-brainer. Because she was a fool to lose her heart to such a man? Same answer.

She'd known it would be bad, but she hadn't expected this crippling pain. Dimly she wondered how she would function, walk and talk, pretend that her world hadn't fallen apart. She imagined this was how it felt to receive a mortal wound. Only her body hadn't registered it yet because it was in shock.

She felt the ache start around her heart, then move in to squeeze. She locked her unhappiness away.

Hot tears rimmed her eyes but didn't fall. They could not ease the throbbing ache that squeezed her heart. Only time could do that. Time and distance.

Lots of time. Lots of distance.

She had survived a cheating fiancé. She'd survive Lucas Reed. She'd survive—even thrive—without him.

The days dragged into a week, then two, and somehow she was dragged along with them. *Passed* was too kind a word for her day-by-day struggle to simply function, Amanda decided, dragging herself from bed.

Thank goodness for her family. At least with them and the demands of running Sweet Bites, she had little opportunity to dwell on her misery.

It was her gift, and her curse, to know her heart so well.

For there would be no other man after Lucas. She might seek companionship, but her heart would remain true. Not out of choice, she admitted, but out of pain.

Lucas had filled the empty places in her life, places she hadn't even known existed . . . until he'd shown her. A soft warmth stole over her as she remembered the tenderness of his kisses.

She needed chocolate. Automatically, she began assembling her ingredients: flour, cocoa, sugar, salt, vanilla, vinegar. She attacked the batter with more force than necessary.

Lucas had loved her wacky cake, she remembered with a pang.

"Lucas." The word was both a plea and a prayer. She didn't realize she'd spoken aloud until she looked up to find Florence and Rudy looking at her, sympathy shining from their eyes.

Flustered, she knocked over the bowl of batter. The bowl shattered, the batter splattering, and Amanda burst into tears.

Florence shooed Rudy out. Amanda sank onto a chair, not caring about the chocolate mess smeared on it. She cradled her head in her palms. The pain couldn't last forever, she assured herself. No more than fifty, sixty years at the most. In time, she would stop yearning for his touch.

A sob erupted before she could stifle it.

In the way of women, Florence had Amanda in her

arms, pressed against her cushiony bosom. "Let out the feelings. Let them all out."

There, in her friend's arms, Amanda forgot about being strong, forgot her need to be in control, forgot everything but the pain that she carried in her heart.

And so she cried. When her sobs subsided into hiccups, she walked over to the mirror and looked at herself. Red-rimmed eyes stared back at her. Okay, she'd had her cry. Now it was time to get on with her life.

"A man who is fighting himself has already lost the battle."

As usual, Florence was right on target. Lucas was fighting himself. Sensing a growing lump in her throat, and knowing that in another moment her friend's sympathy would have her in tears again, Amanda could only nod.

Quietly Florence began cleaning up the mess, stirring Amanda to action.

"I'll do that."

"I thought you might." Looking pleased with herself, Florence wiped off a chair and sank onto it.

Amanda glared at her friend. "I think I've been had."

The older woman looked at her, an innocent expression in her eyes. "Oh?"

Amanda finished wiping off the table and floor. "Yeah." She hugged Florence. "Thanks. I owe you." She tried a smile and found she couldn't make it work. Grief gushed up, hot and bitter, to spill out of her eyes once more. She swiped at the hated tears.

Florence pressed Amanda's hand. "Every man I've

ever known, including The Mister, was a stubborn mule. You just have to show them that you both want the same thing. If he's smart, he'll get it."

Amanda wasn't sure she could speak, that she could push the words up and through her burning throat. "What if he doesn't?"

"Then you kidnap him and make him come to his senses."

She had no idea whether Florence was joking or not. She pressed her fingers to her lips, not certain whether it was to stifle a hysterical desire to laugh or the sob that was perilously close.

"Go after him, honey. It's not just Lucas who needs you. You need him too. We all do."

Amanda knew her friend was only speaking the truth, but the words hurt. A dull ache settled around her heart. "Thanks for caring. But I can't run after him. If Lucas wants me, he knows where to find me."

"You're sure?"

"I'm sure," Amanda said firmly, wishing she believed it.

"You'd know best," Florence said in the tone of one who clearly believed just the opposite. And if Amanda expected her to leave it at that, she didn't know Florence Wanlass.

Chapter Eleven

The washer stopped. Totally, completely stopped. As in never-to-run-again stopped. As in where-was-she going-to-find-the-money-to-buy-a-new-one stopped.

Amanda turned off the main water valve. In a few months, she'd have saved enough to buy a new washing machine, but what was she going to do until then? Every cent she earned at the moment was put back into Sweet Bites.

A tubful of sudsy water and dripping clothes awaited her.

Two hours later, with Florence's help, Amanda hung the last sheet on the line. Even the beauty of an early-autumn day couldn't lift her spirits. Drifts of russet and amber climbed the foothills. Cottonwoods were in that indecisive state, neither green nor gold but somewhere in between. Maples and ashes provided occasional slashes of red.

"Thanks for the help," she said.

"You're welcome, honey." Florence huffed a bit as she made her way to the porch and settled on the swing.

Amanda shoved the rest of the clothespins back into the basket and hurried over to sit by her friend. She should never have allowed Florence to stand out in the sun hanging clothes. Her face was unnaturally flushed, and her breath came in sharp puffs.

"Are you all right?"

"Just have to catch my breath." Florence gave an annoyed grunt. "Getting old is for the birds. And even they don't like it. Time was I could do twenty loads and not raise a sweat when I worked in the laundry in Reno. After I married The Mister, I gave up dealing. It didn't look good, him being on the force and all."

Her breathing had slowed, and Amanda sighed in relief. If anything happened to Florence . . . "Let's go inside. You can lie down and—"

"Not yet. I have something to tell you," Florence said, sounding unaccustomedly nervous. "I wanted to wait, what with you feeling so down and all, but as Rudy said, at our age, we don't have time to be waiting."

Amanda's eyebrows pinched together as she tried to follow the convoluted sentence. "Wait for what?"

"Rudy asked me to marry him." A pretty blush stained the rouged cheeks.

Of course. The guilty looks they exchanged when she saw them holding hands. The way Florence's eyes lit up when Rudy walked into a room. His new energy and enthusiasm for life. If she hadn't been so caught up in her own misery, she'd have seen the signs earlier.

"I'm so happy for you." Amanda gave her friend a quick hug.

"I hoped you'd feel that way."

"Why wouldn't I . . ." Realization came and, with it, a flash of shame. "I've been pretty wrapped up in myself lately, haven't I?"

"Just a bit." Florence's smile softened the sting of the words.

"I'm sorry."

"Hush. You've got no call to feel sorry. You're hurting. And heartache's the worst kind of hurt there is."

Amanda blinked back tears at the understanding in her friend's eyes. Tears gathered in Florence's eyes as well. "Look at us. Blubbering away like a couple of watering cans."

Amanda managed a smile. "No more tears," she promised. "Except happy ones."

"Lucas Reed ought to be horsewhipped," Florence said.

The jolt Amanda felt upon hearing Lucas' name hadn't lessened over the last two weeks. She held up a hand. "Lucas is out of the picture. Besides," she added with a trace of a smile, "we're talking about your life. Not mine."

To Amanda's surprise, Florence blushed. "Do you think we're silly old fools? Marrying at our age."

"Do you love him?"

"With all my heart, and he says he loves me. There're no wrinkles on my soul. Or my heart. Inside"—she tapped her chest—"inside, I feel like a young girl, giddy with her first love."

A pang of envy shot through Amanda. She squelched it as best she could. "I think it's wonderful. Have you decided when?"

"As soon as we can arrange it."

"Would you like to have it here?"

"Nothing would make me happier. You know neither of us has any family to speak of outside of you and each other. I was hoping you'd be my maid of honor."

"I'd love to. We can decorate the house and—"

"We were thinking of having it outside. What do you think of a garden wedding?"

"I think it sounds beautiful," Amanda said, a little catch in her voice.

They spent the next hour making plans. Her earlier sadness melted away as she rejoiced in her friends' happiness, and her battered heart felt better than it had since Lucas had left.

"We'd like to stay right here if it's all right with you," Florence said. "This is our home."

"We'd never leave you," Rudy, who had now joined them, added.

"Maybe we could knock down a wall between the bedrooms and make them into one large room," Amanda said, thinking aloud. "Maybe even put in a bathroom." With Sweet Bites taking off, the budget might stretch by then to include a redecorating job as well.

"That sounds wonderful. We've been wondering how we'd manage the two of us in one room," Florence admitted.

"Didn't worry me," her fiancé said, his eyes sparkling

with mischief. The blush that stained Florence's face made her look like a young girl.

Amanda felt another pang of envy, which she promptly pushed away. The two of them deserved every bit of happiness they could squeeze from life. Despite her resolve, though, she couldn't shake the sense of loss.

She firmly refused Florence's offer to help take down the laundry. The simple task of folding clothes took her mind off her troubles, if only for a short while. When she came to the apron she'd worn when she first admitted to herself her feelings for Lucas, she buried her face in the sun-dried cloth.

She'd been feeling fine, almost normal, until memories of Lucas ambushed her. Would it always be this way?

Impatient with her musings, she closed her eyes, willing the memories away. It didn't matter when it had happened. Or how. Or why. Life had played a cruel trick on her by allowing her to fall in love with the right man who believed he was all wrong for her.

If only . . .

She shook her head. *If only*'s were futile; more than that, they were dangerous. They encouraged you to think about the *might-have-been*s. Her breath caught in a tiny sob as memory after memory of Lucas assailed her.

She missed his wry sense of humor, his sharp insights, even his moods. She had only to close her eyes to recall the feel of his lips on hers, the strength of his arms as they closed around her.

She pushed away the pictures. She didn't have Lucas and never would. She'd honestly thought he'd come to her, that he wouldn't be able to stay away. He loved her. And wherever he was, he loved her still. She believed that with every pore of her being.

Enough, she told herself. She concentrated on what she did have. A home. A family. Love. A soft sob escaped her lips. Just not the love from the one man who'd found his way into her heart.

Despite the pain that squeezed her heart, she smiled faintly, thinking of her family. Rudy and Florence were currently arguing over a card game. One thing was certain: she'd never be bored.

She wandered out to the porch. There was a softness out there that eased some of the pressure from her chest. With a quiet sigh, she let the cool night air swaddle her.

She was taking it a day at a time. It took more effort than she believed possible to get through every day. It was a test of strength and determination. She'd been content before Lucas had found his way into her life, and she'd be content again, after the pain healed.

Though she was functioning, misery still pressed against her heart. If she moved too quickly, let down her guard for an instant, the pain would cripple her.

She pieced together the image of Lucas' face in her mind. She closed her eyes and let it form.

That, too, was a kind of test.

Florence heard the creak of the porch swing. She didn't believe in depending on fairies. She had ideas of her own.

In her room, she pulled out a sheet of stationery. Thirty minutes later, she slid the letter into an envelope.

Lucas Reed, she thought, a self-satisfied smile slipping across her lips, wasn't the only one who knew how to tell a good story.

Four days without a washing machine forced Amanda into approaching the contraption with wrench and screwdriver in hand.

Hours later, she threw both aside, cursed roundly, and failed to convince herself she didn't need another piece of wacky cake.

She slipped into a lavender-scented bath to soak away the morning's frustrations. Her sigh of pleasure was barely a memory when the knock sounded at the door. She sank farther into the tub of scented water. Maybe if she ignored it, whoever it was would go away.

"Amanda," Florence called through the door. "Delivery for you."

This time her sigh was one of frustration. All she'd wanted was to grab a few minutes for herself.

"Can you deal with it?" she yelled back.

" 'Fraid not. The man says he needs your signature."

Regretfully, she rose out of the water, watching as the bubbles popped one by one. "Just a minute." She toweled off and tied her robe around her.

Downstairs, she was still blotting her hair dry. "Okay. What's so important that it couldn't wait ten minutes?"

"This." Florence gestured toward the front door.

A man in a brown service uniform slouched against

the doorjamb. "Washer and dryer, ma'am. Where do you want 'em?"

She looked past him to the yard, where two large cardboard boxes sat. "There's been a mistake. I didn't order these."

"Got the purchase order right here," he said, shoving a form under her nose.

She scanned it before thrusting it back to him. "Look, I didn't buy them. Please take them back."

He pulled a red bandanna from his pocket and wiped the sweat from his neck. "Can't."

"But—"

"Lady," he said in a long-suffering voice. "I can leave 'em in the yard or take 'em inside. Your choice."

She couldn't let him leave expensive appliances in the middle of her yard, not with the sky threatening rain. "Take them around back."

He gave her an approving smile. "Now you're talking."

She scrambled up the stairs, pulled on jeans and a sweatshirt, and hurried back down to the kitchen just as he was wheeling a huge box through the back door.

"Where do you want 'em?"

With the out-of-commission washer occupying the corner, she had no choice but to point to the middle of the kitchen floor.

He gave her a doubtful look. "You sure? I got orders to hook these up and get rid of the old one."

"I'm not going to keep—"

"Lady, this here washer and dryer are bought and paid

for. You gotta keep 'em. Now, where do you want 'em?" His voice strained with impatience.

"I . . . uh . . ."

"I got other deliveries to make today. You planning on keeping me here all day?"

She motioned to the corner. "There. What about the old one?"

"No problem. You still using this antique?" He gave a low whistle, not waiting for her answer. With a minimum of fuss, he hauled away her ancient washer.

She hurried to mop the spot the new appliances would occupy.

He returned in a few minutes with a second box. He stripped away the cardboard packaging and patted the dryer lovingly. "You're getting the best, ma'am. Yes, ma'am, these here are top-of-the-line."

With the same economy of motion he'd used in lugging away the machine, he installed the new ones.

Amanda looked at the gleaming white appliances with panels resembling those of a spaceship. Or a computer. It didn't take much figuring to know who had sent them.

"Thank you for all your trouble."

"My pleasure." With a tip of an imaginary hat, he left.

She walked around the washer and dryer, fingering the array of buttons and knobs. Lucas had bought the best. She tried to see the appliances for what they were: a gift. But her heart wasn't in the mood to accept gifts from a man who couldn't accept the only thing she could give him.

Her love.

A flash of anger surged through her. She welcomed it.

Anger, she understood. Anger, she could deal with. How dare he think he could buy her forgiveness? Well, she'd let him know he couldn't buy his way out of her life.

"Looks like we're moving up in the world," Florence observed.

"What? Oh . . . these. Lucas sent them. He's got another think coming if he thinks he can . . ."

"If he can what?"

"Buy me off."

"You think that's what he's trying to do?"

"I know it is."

"Lucas doesn't strike me as the kind to buy his way out of anything."

The mild censure in her friend's voice had Amanda bristling. "You're siding with him?"

Florence only smiled.

Chapter Twelve

A call from his agent confirmed what Lucas already knew. It was the best work he'd ever done, certain to make the best-seller list, go to paperback, be optioned for motion picture rights. A bidding war was predicted.

Lucas cut off the deluge of words by hanging up.

He rubbed the stubble on his chin. He hadn't shaved that morning. Or the morning before that.

He gazed about the immaculate condo. Not by any stretch of the imagination could it be called a home. It was shelter.

Comfortable, even lavish shelter. But it was only shelter. It wasn't like Amanda's house, where clutter and love mixed together in equal parts. Not for the first time did he find himself missing her . . . and the colorful chaos that comprised her household.

Who'd have thought that he'd miss something as simple and uncomplicated as the companionship of Amanda, Florence, and Rudy, people who'd accepted a loner like him and made him part of their lives?

They had accepted him without question. He didn't have to prove anything to Amanda. All he had to do was love her . . . and accept her love in return.

And therein lay the problem.

He'd actually been thinking about getting a dog. Having a pet would add another heartbeat to the empty rooms, give him companionship. When he realized the direction his thoughts were taking him, he scowled. How pathetic could he get?

He was a big-shot writer. Him, a little orphan kid from nowhere. But it didn't change the loneliness. He could have any woman he wanted—except one.

For a moment . . . only a moment . . . he indulged in a fantasy of Amanda and him together, married. The fantasy dissolved as reality hit him. What did he know about commitment? Or permanence? Or loving and cherishing a woman?

Nothing.

She'd find someone else. Someone who could give her everything she deserved. Someone who wasn't scarred by the past . . . someone who knew how to love.

A picture of Amanda repeating the marriage vows, a white veil and dress highlighting the creaminess of her skin and the fire of her hair, slid into his mind. The image was so vivid, so intense, that he had to shake his head to dispel it.

If he were any kind of a man, he'd be happy for her when she found the man who deserved her. And he would be, he promised himself fiercely. Even if it killed him.

Martyr. The word rang in his head, leaving a bitter aftertaste in his mouth. He was no martyr. So why was he acting like one?

There was an element of pride buried somewhere within all that sackcloth and ashes he insisted on heaping upon himself, pride in his misery.

Suddenly he was tired of both the pride and his self-imposed penitence.

He would always mourn Danny, but it was time to get on with his life. Just as Danny's widow had.

The familiar guilt sank its teeth into him. He hadn't visited Janeen and her son in over a year, despite repeated pleas that he stop by. Before he could talk himself out of it, he called her.

"Lucas!" The genuine pleasure in Janeen's voice warmed him and, perversely, dug the guilt deeper. "It's been too long."

"I know. I'm sorry."

She laughed. "Don't apologize. I know you've been busy writing mongo best sellers." She hesitated. "Could you come by? I've remarried. I'd love for you to meet George."

Lucas started to make excuses, then thought better of it.

"Sure. I'd like that."

"Tonight?"

Why not? "That'd be great." He got directions to her new house and, with a hand to his rough jaw, decided he'd better shower and shave.

An hour later, he found Janeen's house, a bungalow

in a noisy neighborhood of children's squeals and the hum of lawn mowers. A bike leaned against the front porch, a pair of in-line skates propped next to it, along with a Razor skateboard and a football.

She greeted him with a hug. "I'm so glad you came. Dillon missed you. I did too."

Dillon ran into the room, then skidded to a stop. "Uncle Lucas."

Lucas braced himself as Dillon launched his seven-year-old self at him. He lifted the boy to his shoulder and pretended to groan under the slight weight. "Who's this?" he asked Janeen. "This can't be Dillon. He's way too big."

"I'm seven," Dillon announced with the dignity of the very young.

Lucas set Dillon down. "You're right. I won't be making that mistake again."

A tall, balding man joined them. The love in his eyes when he looked at Janeen and Dillon told its own story.

"Lucas, this is my husband, George," Janeen said. "George, Lucas Reed. Danny's partner."

Lucas shook the other man's hand. "Good to meet you."

"Likewise."

The two men took each other's measure. Lucas decided he liked what he saw.

"Hey, pal," George said to Dillon. "What do you say we make ice cream sundaes while your Uncle Lucas is here?"

Dillon gave a hoot of approval and scampered away.

George turned to Lucas. "I'm glad you came. Janeen's been worried about you." He followed Dillon into the kitchen.

"I'm happy for you," Lucas said once he and Janeen were alone. "It looks like you've found yourself a good man."

"I have. I think Danny would have approved."

"I think you're right."

They joined Dillon and his stepfather in the kitchen for sundaes.

"I'm playing Little League baseball," Dillon said. "George is coaching."

George brushed a hand over Dillon's head. "We've got star material here."

Dillon grinned widely, showing a gap in his front teeth.

"George is a great coach!" He looked from one man to the other. "I bet you'd be great at baseball, Uncle Lucas. We could play sometime. If you were around more."

A taut silence stretched among the three adults.

"I know you're real busy," Dillon continued. "Mom says you're writing books about good guys and bad guys. My dad was one of the good guys. Right?"

"Right," Lucas said in a strangled voice.

The sheen of tears glazed Dillon's eyes. "Mom says he was a hero."

"Your mom's right." Lucas' voice grew thick with emotion, and he coughed to clear the huskiness away. "Your dad was a hero."

"I'm going to be a cop when I grow up." Dillon

wrapped his arms around Lucas' neck. "You don't have to worry about not coming by more. Mom says it's because you miss Dad so much and we remind you of him."

"Your mom's a very smart lady."

Once Dillon was out of earshot, Janeen turned to Lucas. "I'd apologize, but he's right." She laid a hand on his and squeezed. "You weren't to blame for what happened to Danny."

What could he say?

"You're a good man, Lucas. Maybe someday you'll start believing that."

George, who had remained silent during the exchange, now spoke up. "You're always welcome here. You're family."

"Thank you. Thank you both."

After making a promise to visit more often, Lucas took his leave and returned to the condo. The emptiness he found there mocked what he'd shared only an hour ago. Loneliness howled through him.

Janeen had clearly moved on with her life. If she could let go of the past, why couldn't he? Janeen had never blamed him for Danny's death, and he knew that Danny himself wouldn't have blamed him. Wasn't that what Amanda had tried to tell him?

What was she doing right now? With Amanda, you never knew. She could be baking another of her decadent delights or playing rummy with Florence or encouraging Rudy with his invention.

A smile touched his lips. He never thought he'd miss

Florence with her turbans and jewels and outlandish suggestions or Rudy with his impossible inventions.

But he did. It came to him then, the truth of it, swirling through his mind and into his heart. He recalled the warm glow in his gut when Amanda had skimmed her hand over his face, had touched her lips to his, had made him part of her life. He loved her. She was light to him when he'd lived in the dark.

There was nothing keeping him in LA. No family. No friends who cared about him more than what he could do for them. No, there was no one to keep him there.

He looked around, trying to find anything he wanted to take with him. That he found nothing other than his laptop was final proof that he was making the right decision.

Life didn't give many second chances, especially to a man who had messed up as royally as he had, but if there was a chance she'd have him, he intended to grab it. He wanted Amanda.

Even more, he needed her.

Chapter Thirteen

Dawn came in a dozen shades of pink and coral, dragging with it a burst of sunshine that gave promise of a beautiful day.

It had been three weeks since Lucas left. Amanda figured she was making progress when she was able to get through a day without breaking down in tears more than once.

After a morning of baking, she took off her apron. "I'm going to work in the garden," she told Florence, "if you're sure you don't need me."

Florence looked up from where she was working on the computer. To the surprise of everyone, including herself, Florence was proving a quick study on the computer and now handled most of the orders.

"You go ahead, honey. We're getting along just fine," she said with a pat to the monitor.

Amanda weeded the rows of vegetables and dead-headed flowers. Working in the dirt, feeling the grit of it

172

beneath her fingernails, lifted her spirits. She inhaled the rich scent of soil and compost.

It was there that Lucas found her, thanks to a tip from Florence.

He stood quietly, not wanting to disturb her. Dirt smudged her face but couldn't obscure the pleasure in her eyes as she worked in the garden.

Once again, he was reminded that Amanda loved with her whole being. She loved nurturing and growing things, whether it be plants or people. Most of all, she loved life. She embraced it with outstretched arms, welcoming both the joy and pain that came with it.

The flowers in her garden, Rudy and Florence—she gave of herself.

Unstintingly.

Unwaveringly.

Unfailingly.

She couldn't have become more beautiful—could she?—in the weeks since he'd left, but it seemed to him, with the sun gilding her hair, that she had.

Her face—the loveliness, the compassion, the strength, and, yes, the vulnerability—was framed by a tumble of curls. He remembered twirling his fingers through those same curls, pulling her to him.

Somehow, Amanda had chosen him. He'd done nothing to deserve the love of such a woman. Still, it was given without reservation, without condition. He'd almost thrown it away with his pigheadedness and pride.

Don't let it be too late, he prayed silently.

Amanda wouldn't fade into the background of his life. She was too vital, too real, too everything, to make her an easy or undemanding companion. But he'd discovered something. He didn't want easy or undemanding.

He wanted Amanda. Just as she was.

He should say something, tell her that he was here. His heart stuttered, robbing him of words. A voice whispered inside his mind to take a chance. Tears stung his eyes as he savored the picture she made surrounded by flowers.

A sweet peace wrapped its way around his heart. He thought of a future with Amanda. There would be laughter. The kind that filled a house and turned it into a home. There'd be tears as well. Life didn't give one without the other. He wanted both, as long as they were shared with her.

Her eyes widened as she took in his presence. For a moment, they warmed with pleasure. It died, and her expression grew guarded. He vowed to change that and said the first thing that came into his mind. "Miss me?"

Amanda rose slowly and gave him an unfathomable stare. "What are you doing here?"

"I had to see you." He paused. "Florence wrote something about a wedding."

"That's right."

He grimaced. She was going to make him sweat. "Who's getting married?"

"Florence and Rudy. Day after tomorrow."

His sigh of relief came out in a whoosh. "That sly old fox."

"Rudy knows how to treat a lady," she said, a faint smile sliding across her lips.

"And I don't?"

She no longer saw ghosts in his eyes, Amanda realized, and hope blossomed within her.

He lowered his head, then kissed her with such burning intensity, she knew he'd missed her every bit as much as she had him.

She melted further into his embrace. The kiss kindled a spiral of pleasure deep within her. She slid her arms around him, letting the needs of the past few weeks take over. His mouth was warm and giving, just as she knew him to be.

"Well?"

Male ego, she thought. What a fragile thing it was. She tilted her head to one side. "Well, maybe you do know how to do some things."

The speculative look in her eyes caused him to stumble for what to say next. "How's the computer working? Did you learn how to run the mailing list? What about—"

"Lucas, did you come all this way to discuss business?"

"Not exactly."

"Why did you come?"

He stalled, looking in her eyes for a hint of what she felt.

Did her response to his kiss mean she'd forgiven him? Or only that she wanted him? Had she stopped loving him? He wouldn't blame her if she had. He'd acted like a world-class jerk. "Don't you know?"

"You'll have to tell me."

He sighed. She wasn't going to make it easy for him. "I came because I couldn't hear the fairies."

"You listened for them?"

He nodded.

"Why?"

Did she have to keep asking that? "Because of you."

"You listened for the fairies because of me? Why?" He heard the smile in her voice.

"Because I love you."

There, he'd said it. The words he'd believed he'd never be able to say, much less mean, rushed from his lips. He pressed those lips to hers.

"I want you. I need you. I was lost without you. A mess. But if, by some miracle, you'll have me . . . if you really meant what you said about . . ."

"Loving you?"

"Yeah. That. Loving me anyway."

"I don't love you anyway. I love you because."

"You were right," he said, determined to get it all out. "I was running away. It feels like I've been running forever. Until you." The admission wasn't as difficult as he'd feared. "I love you," he said again. "I think I knew it that afternoon in the barn. I watched you deliver that calf and knew I would never feel the same way about another woman."

Tears tracked down her cheeks.

"Are you crying?"

"I always cry when I'm happy."

"Does this mean you're going to cry at our wedding?"

Her thoughts scattered like sunbeams caught in the clouds. "Wedding?"

"The one we're going to have tomorrow."

"You're crazy."

"You aren't going to make me wait, are you?"

A bubble of laughter spilled over. "Two weeks. As soon as Florence and Rudy are back from their honeymoon."

"Two weeks," he agreed reluctantly. "But no longer."

"Maybe a little longer," she said, unable to resist teasing him. "We need to invite guests, order a cake, buy a dress—"

"You don't need a dress. You look great just like you are."

She glanced down at her faded jeans and peasant-style blouse. "You really are crazy, you know that?"

"Yeah. About you." He fitted his finger under her chin, tilting it up so that her eyes met his.

"I ought to be angry with you," she said. "About that bribe."

"Bribe?"

"The washer and dryer."

"Washer and dryer?"

"The ones you had delivered."

"You knew it was me?"

She rolled her eyes in exasperation. "Of course I knew."

"Oh."

He looked so sheepish that she laughed.

"They weren't a bribe. Florence wrote that the washing machine died. I knew you needed a new one and that you wouldn't let me buy them for you." He didn't give her a chance to deny it. "I know I'm not a good risk, but I'll do everything I can to make you happy."

"I know," she whispered, her gaze loving him.

"You won't be sorry."

She put a finger to his lips. "How could I?"

"I love you." The words that had refused to come in the past now slipped off his tongue with an ease that still managed to surprise him.

They were as natural as touching her, as easy as breathing.

They weren't planned; they simply were. He said them again and heard the rightness of them, felt the truth he'd been denying.

"I love you." Suddenly, he couldn't say them enough. He wanted to shout them to the world. He wanted to whisper them against her hair.

He kissed her again, a kiss filled with the healing balm of old wounds laid to rest. A kiss filled with a promise for tomorrow and all the tomorrows after that. A kiss with love and trust enough to see them through the bad times as well as the good.

"I'm glad," she said softly.

The tightness in his chest eased a notch. "So am I." He hesitated. "I'm sorry."

She looked up. "I know."

There was no reproach in her eyes, no recriminations in her voice, only acceptance. Once more he was humbled . . . and awed.

He stalled, looking into her eyes for a hint of what she felt. "Don't you want to know why?"

"You'll have to tell me."

He sighed. She wasn't going to make it easy for him. Well, he hadn't expected her to. "I was wrong." The words weren't as difficult to say as he'd feared. And with them he shed the last of the pain, a legacy of the past.

"You had your reasons."

The acknowledgment of his feelings, the quiet acceptance, was more healing than any of the empty words offered by well-meaning friends and acquaintances. Once again, he found himself a recipient of her compassion, her understanding. How had he ever turned away from it? How had he thought, even for a moment, that he could live without her?

Not for the first time, Lucas realized how Amanda had healed the wounds of the past with her simple goodness.

"Will you forgive me?"

In answer, she brought his hand to her lips and pressed a kiss to his palm.

Forgiveness. So easily given and yet so hard to accept. Until now. Until Amanda.

"Thank you," he said in a hoarse whisper, wondering how she had found the grace to forgive him even now, after he'd caused her so much pain.

"Something happened to me," he said. "Maybe it's been happening since the day I met you. The past is who

I was, and I'll never be able to escape it, not completely. But it's not who I am now, who I want to be." His voice turned harsh, as though it might break. "I want to be the man you love. I love you."

There, he'd said it again. He pressed a kiss to her lips.

"Don't," she begged. "Don't say it if you don't mean it. I couldn't bear it. I've learned something about myself during the last weeks."

"What's that?" He was afraid, more afraid than he'd ever been in his life. What if she told him that she no longer wanted to be with him?

"I won't compromise. I won't be with a man who doesn't respect me enough to believe me when I tell him that I love him."

The breath she took trembled out. "I won't be with a man who doesn't have the guts to stick around for the long haul."

Amanda had given it to him with both barrels. He'd expected no less. From the beginning, she'd refused to pander to his ego by letting him get away with excuses or half-truths. Wasn't that one of the reasons he loved her as he did?

"I love you," he said again. "I know you love me. I've never meant anything more."

She melted into his embrace.

He touched his lips to her temples, kissing them each in turn before turning his attention to her mouth. "I don't deserve you."

She raised laughing eyes to his. "You're right. You don't."

He stared, then gave a snort of laughter. That was his Amanda. Always ready to put him in his place. And he loved her for it. He took her hand, raised it to his lips, and kissed her fingertips.

Her eyes turned serious. "You have everything that's important." She placed a hand on his heart. "Here."

He gave himself up to the promise in her voice, the love shining from her eyes.

His arms came around her, tentatively at first, then more firmly. Holding her again was a miracle.

He slanted his lips over hers, remembering the first time he'd kissed her. It was just as it had been, and it was nothing like it. This time he knew how he would feel, what he would want, when he kissed her. He knew, and still he was stunned.

Stunned by the love with which she returned it. Stunned by his own need to give back. Stunned by the realization that nothing would ever matter, could ever matter, as much as the fact that he loved her and she loved him. Whatever their differences—and there were plenty—that wouldn't change.

He'd known. Of course he'd known that he loved her, but nothing equaled the reality of having her in his arms. Nothing equaled the satisfaction of loving her and knowing this was only the beginning.

A tear slipped through her lashes. Lucas caught it on the tip of his thumb and brought it to his lips. "I won't promise there won't be any more tears, but I can promise that I'll always be there to wipe them away."

"I love you."

"And I love you right back."

They would have a future, he thought. There'd be children and grandchildren. They'd grow old together. Laugh and cry, argue and make up—they'd do all that and more.

His gaze settled on her, and he caught his breath. He thought he would drown in the love he saw reflected in her eyes.

How had he, with all his weaknesses and sins, found such a woman? She was light and life, breath and being to him. He no longer really worried that he didn't deserve her. Love wasn't earned. It wasn't bought with good deeds. It was given, freely. As Amanda's was.

And he, with more than his share of sins, had received the greatest gift of all.

Amanda.

Epilogue

The wedding was beautiful in its simplicity. The only hitch occurred when Harry found the Champagne Lucas had ordered and managed to knock a bottle off the counter, lapping up its contents. He hiccupped through the ceremony.

Lucas felt a knot form in his throat as he looked at Amanda, radiant in a dress the color of lilacs with flowers woven through her hair.

Listening to the couple recite their vows, he pictured himself and Amanda repeating the same words. The image was so vivid that he was jolted back to reality only when the minister asked who gave the bride in marriage.

"I do," Lucas said, his voice little more than a croak. He wondered how he got the words out at all and tried again. "I do."

A wad of emotion filled his throat as he watched the rest of the ceremony. His gaze caught Amanda's. And held. The love that shone in her eyes was as real a force as any other in nature. That he'd spent so much time denying it filled him with shame.

The minister completed the rites, finishing with, "You may now kiss the bride."

The newlyweds kissed to the cheers of the onlookers.

That evening, after seeing Rudy and Florence off on a honeymoon to Bimini—Lucas' treat—he and Amanda settled on the porch swing. He remembered another evening, where he'd given in to the impulse to kiss Amanda. Love pulsed through him now as he touched his lips to hers.

"Only another week," she said, her husky voice turning his insides to marshmallow.

"An eternity."

The night enfolded them, the stars sparkling like diamonds against a sky of black velvet.

Her hand found his. "Listen."

He did as she bade and heard a soft, clear tune, like that of a flute. The breeze whispered an accompaniment.

"The fairies are happy for us," she whispered.

Lucas had no trouble believing it at all.